THE TRUTH ABOUT THE ROGUE

WHISPERS OF THE TON (BOOK 2)

ROSE PEARSON

© Copyright 2024 by Rose Pearson - All rights reserved.

In no way is it legal to reproduce, duplicate, or transmit any part of this document by either electronic means or in printed format. Recording of this publication is strictly prohibited and any storage of this document is not allowed unless with written permission from the publisher. All rights reserved.

Respective author owns all copyrights not held by the publisher.

THE TRUTH ABOUT THE ROGUE

PROLOGUE

Scowling, Andrew Whitfield, Marquess of Kentmore, crumpled up the piece of paper and threw it onto the floor, letting it sit with the ever-growing pile of rejected pieces. The words were not coming to him and yet, he had a great desire to write and to write well. It was foolishness to become so tied up in such a thing, but Andrew could not resist the literary urge.

"If only my words would make sense," he muttered, as he shoved one hand through his hair and, after another sigh, picked up his quill again. Closing his eyes, he considered the young lady he had held in his arms only a few hours ago at the ball, reminding himself of the sweetness of her smile, of the bright light in her green eyes, of the color in her cheeks as he had swept her around the floor. That had brought him a great deal of satisfaction, of course, knowing that his presence was the cause of her flushed cheeks and warm smile but, all the same, it had not brought him what he was looking for.

"Which is why it is near enough impossible to

describe it," he muttered to himself, looking down at the blank piece of paper. Yes, he could write about the beauty of a lady's face, the interest that had filled him when he had first seen her but, given that he had never experienced anything more than that, Andrew could not easily describe what it felt like to have a strong or growing affection. More than that, he could not talk about what it was like to be in love, to have one's heart touched by a sweetness that filled one's entire being – but what he *could* write of was the desire for such a thing. He could write about longing, about a strong and unyielding desire for something more, for something so profound, there would not be words to describe it.

Sighing, Andrew dipped his quill in the ink and began to write, his poetry spreading out across the page, speaking of desire, hope, and eagerness, using the young lady he had danced with as his muse. When it was complete, he set the quill down, read it again, read it a second time, and with a small shrug, picked up the sand to dry the ink.

It was not perfection, of course, for he was never truly satisfied with all that he had written, but it was enough.

"Not that I truly desire to fall in love and marry," he muttered to himself, rolling up the paper carefully. "That would take me away from the life I have at present – a life which I very much enjoy!"

With a smirk, he sat back in his chair and thought about the young lady he had danced with, how he had held her tight in his arms, seen her gaze up at him with hope-filled eyes, and how, thereafter, he had managed to steal a kiss from her in the shadows of the ballroom. He would do no more, of course, given that she was a proper young lady who had only just come out, but that did not mean that he could not – and would not – do the same again, with any other young ladies of his acquaintance.

"Kentmore?"

Hastily, Andrew picked up the roll of paper and, opening one of his drawers, set it in there and then closed it tightly.

"Stockton?"

"Yes, it is I. I did say that I would bring my carriage to collect you, to demand that you attend with us, did I not?" The gentleman who half-staggered, half-fell into the room grinned rather vaguely at Andrew who immediately laughed and rose from his chair. "Though I must say that your butler was a little unwilling to let me in to see you."

"That is because it is late, and I had already stated that I was to retire." Andrew moved around from his desk and put his hand on his friend's shoulder. "I shall join you at White's another evening."

"Ah, but we are not to go to White's any longer," the gentleman replied, making Andrew's eyebrows lift in surprise. "Lord Stewart – the Baron, you know, but very wealthy with it – has a soiree this evening to which, I know, Lady Beatrice has been invited."

That gave Andrew pause.

"Lady Beatrice?"

His friend chuckled a little darkly.

"Yes, indeed. And the recently widowed Lady Edmunton."

"I see." Andrew ran one hand over his chin. "Well,

that does change things, does it not?"

"I thought that it might, yes," came the slightly slurred reply. "Now, shall you join us, or will you remain home and retire to bed?"

Hearing the hint of a sneer in the gentleman's voice, Andrew's smile faded, only to rush back to him as he thought of Lady Edmunton. She was a widow, and *very* eager indeed for his company whenever he wished it, and tonight, Andrew considered, he might very well desire her presence also.

"Yes, I think I shall attend."

"Capital!"

"For what good is being a rogue if I cannot make my presence known at as many soirees and balls as possible?" Andrew grinned, turning and leading his friend back towards the door, relieved that his poetry was safely hidden away. "I have no doubt that there will be an expectation of my presence, mayhap!"

Lord Stockton laughed aloud.

"Quite right! And you would disappoint society if you did not attend," he said, bolstering Andrew's desire to attend this soiree. "I am delighted that you are to come with us, old boy. It will be a very enjoyable evening, I am sure."

Already thinking of the way that he might pull Lady Edmunton close, or flirt with the young Lady Beatrice - who had been showing him a great deal of interest of late - Andrew found himself grinning.

"Yes, indeed," he answered, his eyes alight with sudden anticipation. "I think that it shall be a very enjoyable evening indeed."

CHAPTER ONE

"Must you always be reading?"

Charlotte, already irritated by her sister's presence, looked up.

"It is not whether I must or not. It is whether I desire to or not."

"And yet, you *always* appear to desire to do so." Lillian sighed and sat down in the chair opposite Charlotte, rolling her eyes as though Charlotte had done something wrong in choosing to read. "Must you be so dull? We shall never find husbands if you pull back from society."

"Given that you are a year older than I, and are expected to find a husband first, I hardly think that my reading is a concern of yours," Charlotte answered, a little hotly given her increasing frustration. "You may prefer dances and soirees and the like, but I do not."

Her sister yawned widely and then rolled her eyes for a second time.

"You would be much better spending time out in

society rather than sitting at home with a book or playing the pianoforte. I did hear Mama say that she was greatly surprised that you did not want to attend the fashionable hour yesterday."

Charlotte scowled, setting her book aside.

"But if my mother did not see the need to force me to attend, then I am surprised that *you* think you must speak to me about it. What difference does it make to you if I read? Why should you be concerned if I prefer to practice the pianoforte rather than wander around the park during the fashionable hour?"

"Because," her sister replied, spreading out her hands and speaking slowly as though Charlotte was foolish in her lack of understanding, "it bears an influence upon our family. When a gentleman considers a lady, they do consider the entire family which includes you, my dear sister. If you are a quiet mouse of a creature, then the gentlemen of London might think that *I* am the same, and will never consider me because of it."

Now it was Charlotte's turn to roll her eyes.

"I am certain that such a thing would never be, given that it is clear from the very first moment of introduction to you that you are... eager in your conversation and the like, Lillian."

This made her sister scowl, her brow furrowing.

"Do you mean to say that I am overeager? Improper, somehow?"

Charlotte quickly shook her head, though inwardly, she considered how her sister had behaved of late. They had only attended two balls and one soiree as yet, but Lillian had been most fervent in her hopes of becoming acquainted with as many gentlemen as she could. Every time that one had drawn near, Lillian had dropped into a curtsy without so much as a word of introduction, obvious in her hope that this gentleman would then be impressed with her propriety and would come to speak with her. That, however, had not occurred. Once their mother, Viscountess Morton, had bade Lillian to stop that behavior, Lillian had then gone on to speak with far too much eagerness when new acquaintances had been made. Indeed, Charlotte had found herself feeling a little sorry for the gentlemen who had come to speak with them, for they had struggled to get a word in anywhere!

"I am much better in society than you shall ever be," Lillian declared, haughtily. "I may be fervent in my desire to speak to the gentlemen and ladies of London, but it is better to be so than to hide yourself away and appear of little interest to anyone!"

Charlotte tried not to say anything in response, even though her heart twisted painfully at her sister's description of her. To Charlotte's mind, she was not in the least bit dull but, evidently, Lillian herself thought so. She closed her eyes for a moment as she took a long breath and then turned her attention back to her book, hearing Lillian's huff of breath. Ignoring this, Charlotte tried to concentrate on what she was reading but the words did not seem to make sense to her. Over and over again, she read the same sentence before, finally, giving up.

"Is there a reason that you are here with me, Lillian?" she asked, pointedly, as her sister rolled one curl lightly around her finger and then released it. "Is there some reason that you are sitting with me instead of preparing yourself for afternoon calls?"

"I am ready," Lillian answered, gesturing with her other hand toward Charlotte. "You, however, appear to have chosen one of your oldest and least interesting gowns from your wardrobe. Do you not see that yellow is a color that does not suit you? Your hair is much too fair for that. Instead, you ought to choose something that makes a gentleman notice your hair color, which then might let his gaze stray to your eyes."

Charlotte closed her eyes.

"Lillian, please. I am quite contented in what I am wearing, I assure you."

"But it is not suitable!"

The door opened just as Lillian finished speaking, and their mother swept into the room, her gaze going straight to Lillian.

"What is not suitable, my dear?"

Lillian gestured to Charlotte directly, one hand sweeping downwards.

"The gown she is wearing! It is not in the least bit suitable, for the gentlemen who will come to call will not think well of her at all! That color makes her appear sickly, does it not? I think that a gown of ivory, or mayhap of light blue, might do a good deal better."

Charlotte said nothing, her gaze going to her mother, who was looking at her with what Charlotte took to be sympathy lingering in her gaze. It seemed that the Viscountess was very much aware of the difference between her daughters and was not particularly pleased with all that Lillian was saying.

"I think that Lillian, while you may be correct in suggesting that the color of gown that Charlotte wears is not ideal, given her complexion and fair curls, you have not chosen the best way to say such things," came the reply, making Charlotte's shoulders round just a little, somewhat disappointed that her mother was agreeing with Lillian. "Charlotte, if that is the gown that you have chosen, then you need not concern yourself with going to change into something else, even though doing so might be desirable. The afternoon calls will begin soon, we hope, and I am sure that whichever gentlemen come to call, they will not find anything to dislike about either of you." She smiled warmly and Charlotte nodded, though her spirits continued to sink. "Lillian, I presume that you are prepared?"

"Of *course* I am, Mama," Lillian answered, quickly. "I have spent a great deal of time preparing."

"Very good." Without making any further remark, Lady Morton sat down and then looked directly to Charlotte. "You will have to put your book away when the gentlemen come to call, as we hope they will."

Charlotte nodded.

"I am aware of that, Mama."

"What I have also come to tell you both is that there are to be no interactions with any gentleman who calls himself a rogue, nor whom the *ton* finds disgraceful in any way, do you understand?"

Lillian drew herself up.

"I should never even *think* to go near to such a gentleman, Mama! I am surprised that you even need to ask me such a thing."

Lady Morton smiled gently, taking no offense at her daughter's reaction.

"My dear, you are young and naïve, and I must explain this to you in clear, succinct terms."

Charlotte frowned.

"Explain what, Mama?"

"That the rogues of London do not always appear to *be* rogues," her mother said, gently. "There are those in London society who seem to be just as every gentleman ought to be. They are polite, well-mannered, and genteel, and will ask you to dance on occasion. However, given the opportunity, they might well try to pull you into their arms, might try to tug you this way and that, and can risk your reputation in doing so."

"But I would never give in," Lillian declared, stoutly, as Charlotte nodded in agreement with her. "I would never permit any gentleman to steal me away from your side when I ought not to."

"Nor would I," Charlotte protested, though their mother only smiled and shook her head.

"My dears, you say such a thing at this moment, but you cannot know for certain. What if that gentleman has shown you a great deal of interest? What if his pleas soften your heart? You may say now, at this moment, that you would do nothing, but I can promise you, your heart can be changed very quickly indeed." Rather than protest, Charlotte chose to remain silent and consider what her mother had said, even though her desire was to insist that she would never do such a thing as that. She looked to Lillian who was frowning heavily, clearly determining that she would not allow any gentleman to steal her away but choosing, as Charlotte was doing, to keep that to herself for the time being. "I know of three gentlemen that you must not draw near," their mother continued, still speaking gently. "Lord Remmington, Lord Freetown, and Lord Ponsonby. There are others, I am sure, but for the moment, these three gentlemen are not to be given any of your attention."

"I understand, Mama," Charlotte murmured, as Lillian chimed in with an agreement of her own. "I will be careful."

"Good." Lady Morton took a breath, then settled back a little more in her chair. "Now, all we must do is wait – and hope – that some gentlemen will come to call."

Charlotte glanced at her sister, who was looking at her with a slightly arched eyebrow as though questioning whether or not Charlotte would do as both her mother and Lillian herself had suggested and go to change her gown. With a lift of her chin, Charlotte folded her hands in her lap and gazed back steadily at Lillian, refusing to be moved.

"*Please*, Charlotte!" Lillian exploded in a sudden fit of emotion, waving her hands around wildly. "This is of the greatest importance to me, and you look so pale that you appear unwell! The gown is not suitable, and you know that you have a good many others in your wardrobe. Why will you not change?"

"I do not need to. This is entirely suitable."

"I am aware that it is suitable, but it does not *suit* you," Lillain exclaimed, just as the tea tray was brought in and set in front of them. "Please, Charlotte. I am aware that any gentlemen who come to call will be coming to see me rather than you, but all the same—"

"Lillian!" Lady Morton exclaimed as Lillain ducked her head, her cheeks flushing hot. "How could you say such a thing to Charlotte?"

"But you know it is true, Mama," Lillian protested weakly as Charlotte too dropped her gaze, her face hot, though it was with the mortification of being spoken to so, as well as a faint trace of anger which ran through her. "I am not speaking lies."

Lady Morton lifted her chin.

"You cannot tell one gentleman's determinations from another, Lillian," she said firmly, "and nor can you speak with such unkindness! Now, pour the tea and do not say any more of such things. I am displeased with you. If Charlotte wishes to wear that gown, then that is her decision – and if she wishes to read a book rather than attend the fashionable hour, I shall not force the matter. You are both very different creatures and that is quite all right. One is not better than the other, I can assure you, and it is my firm hope that you will each find a gentleman who not only understands the character you are, but also adores everything about you."

Charlotte smiled at her mother, feeling a sense of relief lift her.

"Thank you, Mama. It brings me great relief to know that you value that in me."

Her mother smiled back at her.

"Of course I do."

"Though," Lillian protested, getting up to pour the tea, "that does still mean that Charlotte must consider how to first garner the attention of such gentlemen, does it not?"

Their mother frowned.

"Lillian."

"You know what I mean, Mama," Lillian continued, blithely. "She will not be seen by the gentlemen of London if she does not step out into society!"

"I do step out into society," Charlotte answered, sharply, her anger beginning to rise as Lillian offered her a small, tight smile. "Simply because I do not desire the fashionable hour does not mean that society does not know me."

Lady Morton nodded.

"Precisely."

"But there is also the presentation of our family that Charlotte must consider," Lillian continued, refusing, it seemed, to drop the issue. "To have her so pale and so quiet might make the *ton* think that we are both of the same dull nature and then they will not come near to me! The least Charlotte could do would be to wear her most complimentary gowns."

Charlotte closed her eyes as anger burned up through her chest.

"Lillian, will you *please* desist? I am not going to change my gown, despite your protestations. I think that what I am wearing is perfectly suitable and – oh!"

Lillian immediately cried an apology, but it was much too late for that. The cup of tea she had been holding, the one she had been making to set in front of Charlotte, had somehow tipped and the contents had splashed all over Charlotte's gown.

"Lillian! For heaven's sake!" Their mother got to her feet at once, taking Charlotte's hand to pull her up from her chair. "Charlotte, are you quite all right? That tea was very hot."

"I am well," Charlotte answered, her heart pounding as the anger she had felt now began to turn to fury. "Lillian, you did that purposefully!"

"I did nothing of the sort," Lillian exclaimed, her hands going to her hips. "It was an accident, that is all."

"I hardly think so," Charlotte answered, narrowing her eyes. "You were so determined that I should change my gown that you have forced my hand!"

She heard Lillian's protests of innocence but, at the same time, saw the flickering smile that Lillian tried so hard to hide.

"There is nothing to be done but for you to go and change," Lady Morton said, sighing and passing one hand across her eyes. "Lillian, though you have said it was an accident, I must hope that you are speaking the truth." She paused for a moment as if to give Lillian time to announce that no, she had not been telling the truth in stating it had been done accidentally, but Lillian only sat down again in her chair and reached for her teacup. Charlotte's fury rose to even greater heights, and, for a moment, she thought about sitting down again and refusing to move, even with her gown being as it was. "Please, Charlotte," her mother continued, sounding rather weary. "I know that you did not want to do so but please, go and change your gown. The gentlemen callers will be here very soon, and I do not want you to miss any of them."

Charlotte saw the hint of a smile linger on Lillian's face and heard the words whisper back again in her mind.

"I am sure that Lillian can do very well without me," she said, her voice a little hoarse, such was her frustration which, now, was beginning to turn to upset. "Do excuse me."

She did not heed her mother's call, did not listen to the words encouraging her to come back just as soon as she could. Instead, Charlotte picked up her book and hurried from the room, rushing upstairs to her bedchamber where, finally, she found a little solace. The anger she had felt take hold of her when Lillian had first spilled the tea on her gown had quickly faded, leaving Charlotte now with nothing but hot tears and a heart that ached. Yes, she was different from her sister, yes, she was markedly altered in what concerned her as opposed to what concerned Lillian, but did her sister have to take that with such seriousness? Charlotte had never imagined that Lillian's determination to have her change her gown would reach such a fervor!

"I am sure that there will be at least one gentleman who will take note of me," she mumbled, going to ring the bell so that her maid might come to help her change her gown. "Even if I do not particularly care about the color of my gown." Try as she might, Charlotte could not rid herself of the words her sister had said about her, and could not hide the pain that those words had caused. She sat down on the edge of her bed and clutched at her book, closing her eyes and feeling dampness on her lashes. Despite all that Lillian might think, Charlotte did truly want to find herself a suitable match, albeit not in the way that Lillian herself thought to go about things. It was as their mother had said - Charlotte wanted a gentleman who would not only know all about her but would think well of all the different parts of herself that made up her character. She did not ask for, nor even imagine, that love might ever be a part of her future, but all the same, to have someone who would treat her with kindness and appreciation was something she could not set aside. "I want to have a gentleman by my side who will not expect me to be more than I am," she breathed to herself, opening her eyes and wiping away the tears before the maid arrived. "Someone who will value my love of reading, someone who will accept the quietness of my demeanor." Taking a deep breath, she closed her eyes again and squeezed them tightly shut, the pain in her heart burning all the more fiercely.

Though mayhap such a thing will never be possible, and I shall end up alone.

CHAPTER TWO

"Good afternoon, my friend."
Andrew straightened from where he had been bowing over Lady Bradford's hand, only to grin broadly and drop the hand immediately, turning away from her at once.

"Glenfield! How good to see you!" The clearing of a throat caused him to pause and turn back to Lady Bradford, who was now looking at him with a slightly lifted eyebrow. "Forgive me," he said quickly, having no desire to lose her interest in him, "but I must step away. Lord Glenfield has only just returned to London, it seems, and I have not seen him in some months! I shall return and steal more of your time for myself, however. Very soon, I assure you."

This brought a small smile to the lady's face, and she gave him both a nod and a touch of her fingers to his before she stepped away. When Andrew looked back to his friend, Lord Glenfield was grinning broadly.

"I see that you have the same intentions this Season

as you did last Season?" he asked, as Andrew chuckled. "Might I ask who that lady was?"

"A lady whose husband has disappeared to the continent and has not returned as yet, even though he has been away a year!" Andrew shrugged. "If she wishes for a bit of attention, I cannot blame her for that, now can I?"

He lifted his eyebrows, and his friend laughed aloud, slapping Andrew on the back.

"You certainly have not changed in the least!" he exclaimed, as both he and Andrew made their way to the other side of the room, with Andrew spying the table where a footman waited to dispense glasses of whisky and brandy. "I, however, have decided that I must change."

This stopped Andrew short.

"I beg your pardon?"

He looked back at his friend steadily, though Lord Glenfield merely shrugged and then reached for two glasses, pushing one into Andrew's hand.

"I have decided that I must change," Lord Glenfield said again, more steadily this time. "I have been something of a rogue for the last few Seasons – though nothing like you! – and I have determined that I shall be a rogue no more." Something cold seemed to drape itself around Andrew's shoulders. He had expected Lord Glenfield to be just the same as he had been before, determined to make as much of a nuisance of himself as he could. He had expected Lord Glenfield to be as much of a rogue as he had ever been though, certainly, he had been a little less so than Andrew, but to know that he would change entirely was not something that Andrew had been prepared for. "You need not look so disappointed!" Laughing, Lord Glenfield shrugged. "I will be just as I was with you before, at least. Our friendship will be the same as it has always been!"

"I am glad to hear that at least," Andrew answered, trying to rearrange his expression so he did not look as sorrowful. "Might I ask what precisely it is that you mean?"

His friend smiled.

"I mean that I intend to marry."

Andrew sucked in a breath, the future he had anticipated shattering into a thousand pieces. He had known that Lord Glenfield had been considering his responsibilities last Season, but had never expected that *this* would be the answer he would come up with! To consider matrimony was one thing, but to pursue it was quite another and Andrew had expected many a Season ahead of them where they would both continue on just as they pleased. Evidently, his expectation had been quite wrong.

"I do not have any young lady in mind as yet," his friend continued, as though this was just as Andrew ought to have expected, "but all the same, I do not think that it will be too difficult to discover someone. The London Season is just as it should be in that, is it not?"

"If by that, you mean that it is filled with young ladies, all with the hope of finding themselves a husband, then yes, I would say that you are quite right there," Andrew admitted, albeit a little ruefully. "Though I myself would have no interest in such a thing."

"No?" His friend chuckled. "I thought you might have changed your mind, given your... other hobby."

"Hush!" Andrew exclaimed, leaning closer to his friend, fright making his heart leap in his chest. "You know very well that I do not speak of that to anyone. You are the only one who is aware of it."

Lord Glenfield's expression became suddenly serious, and he put one hand to his heart.

"Forgive me, I ought not to have made light of that," he said, with a genuineness that Andrew took to be real. "I know that it is a great secret, and I will always be grateful to you for taking me into your confidence."

Andrew studied his friend's expression, decided that Lord Glenfield appeared genuine, and then nodded, looking away. It had only been last Season that Lord Glenfield had accidentally discovered Andrew's love of writing verse, though he had initially believed that it had been poetry sent *to* Andrew rather than Andrew writing it himself. It had been an awkward moment, but Andrew had ultimately decided that he would tell his closest friend the truth, given that they were the very best of friends and because he knew that he could trust him.

And I can trust him still.

"I presume that you are still pursuing that particular endeavor?"

Andrew nodded, glancing around him for fear that someone would overhear.

"Yes, I am."

"And have you thought to publish it anywhere?"

Andrew blinked.

"Publish?"

"Yes, publish," Lord Glenfield repeated with a smile. "I saw recently that The London Chronicle was seeking new articles to go into their publication. I am certain that, should you send your work there, it would be printed, and all of the *ton* would read it."

Andrew quickly shook his head.

"I have no interest in having anyone from society reading my work."

"Though," his friend suggested with a smile, "you could send it in anonymously, could you not?"

Hesitating, the protest dying away on his lips, Andrew considered his friend's suggestion.

"I – I suppose that I might."

"It would be interesting to see the response from the *ton*, would it not?"

A corner of Andrew's lips turned up.

"Or might it be that *you* would like to use my published work to elicit the attention of particular young ladies?" Seeing his friend flush and look away, Andrew laughed aloud. Lord Glenfield had always bemoaned his lack of ability when it came to writing sonnets and the like, though previously, they had always been written to garner the attention from young ladies for the sole purpose of their own entertainments rather than for stealing their hearts. Now, however, Andrew suspected that Lord Glenfield might wish to use the published work to read aloud to any young lady he had set his eyes upon and, given the way that his friend would not look at him, Andrew believed himself to be correct. "That is not a bad thing, my friend though, if you like, I could write you your own sonnets, with which you could entrance whichever young lady you set your mind upon."

With a scowl, Lord Glenfield shook his head.

"Though I might find the written verse difficult, I cannot – and will not – use your work to engage the interest of any young lady, for that would be a falsehood," he stated unequivocally. "I am quite serious about this, Kentmore. I will not have a young lady drawn to me who believes that I am capable of writing beautiful words of love and devotion when I have no gift in that whatsoever."

"But all the same," Andrew added, refusing to be dissuaded, "if my work was published, then you might be able to read it with great feeling and affection, drawing the young ladies of London to you." He reached out his hands as he spoke, then pulled his hands in towards himself. "That would be a good thing, surely?"

His friend's lips quirked.

"Mayhap," he admitted, shrugging. "But you must first consider whether or not you *will* publish your work. Though I might want to use it for my own purposes, I can assure you that I believe that it is worthy enough, in its own right, to be published! I am also quite certain that the *ton* would think very highly of it and, no doubt, might be eager to hear more."

Andrew considered this, then tilted his head.

"I suppose then that I could use it to my own advantage also," he said, slowly, as Lord Glenfield frowned in obvious confusion. "I could take the poetry and read it to whichever young lady *I* was focusing on at the time, could I not?" He chuckled as Lord Glenfield rolled his eyes but grinned. "I might consider it. The London Chronicle, you say?" Seeing his friend nod, Andrew ran one hand over his chin, feeling himself grow more and more contented with the idea. "Then I think I shall. Thank you for that, Glenfield. I expect my first poem to be out amongst the *ton* very soon!"

∼

'IN FIELDS OF GOLD, *where wildflowers throng,*
 Love's gentle breeze whispers its song
 As we walk, hand in hand, our embrace so sweet,
 Our lips, our hearts, our lives, now meet.
 A love, a flame that burns so bright,
 Will guide us through the dark of night.
 Our love, so strong, will forever shine,
 A love so pure, so true, so divine.'

Andrew smiled to himself as he sat back in his carriage, his satisfaction continuing to grow as he considered each and every word. It had only been a short poem, yes, but it had been enough for him to send to The London Chronicle in the hope that they would publish it.

And publish it they had, albeit with the word, 'Anon' at the bottom, just as he had requested. He had been very cautious indeed in how he had gone about sending the poem into the Chronicle in the first place, taking it with him into the heart of London and, thereafter, paying a ragamuffin handsomely to have it delivered. The child would not know who he was so, therefore, there was not even the smallest suspicion that anyone would recognize him. This was just as he had desired, just as he had hoped for and, now, to see his work printed did bring Andrew a good deal of contentment.

I should thank Lord Glenfield for his suggestion, he

thought to himself, as the carriage rolled its way toward St James' Park. *And mayhap send in another one very soon.*

The carriage stopped and Andrew climbed out, ready to take a stroll through the park and see who he might engage in either conversation, or perhaps in something a little more intimate. Placing his hat on his head, he strode directly into the park, only to come to an abrupt stop.

How very strange.

There were clusters of ladies all standing about together, their heads bent forward as though they were whispering to one another. Andrew could not understand it, frowning heavily as he began to make his way towards one of the small groups, confused as to why so many young ladies were standing in such a way.

"A love so divine," he heard one of them murmur, his heart quickening as he realized what it was that the lady was speaking of. "I do wonder who it is that this gentleman is writing about."

"Mayhap it is a great secret," said another, a wistfulness in her voice. "Mayhap he is much too overcome with love for her to be able to express it in any other way than this. Mayhap there is a reason that they cannot be together, and this is the only way for him to speak with her."

A small, collective sigh ran around the group and Andrew, who had slowed his steps to a mere crawl to listen, grinned broadly, ducking his head so that the ladies would not see his expression. They were speaking of the poem, he realized, his heart suddenly soaring. They not only appreciated it, they thought well of it and, seemingly, were losing themselves in raptures about what was said within it - which was, Andrew considered, precisely what he had hoped for.

Though, a little voice said in his mind, *you know nothing of love. All you speak of is imagined, all you write comes from what you believe love might be like. There is no truth in that.*

With a shake of his head, Andrew dismissed that thought and, lifting his gaze, continued to walk through the park, taking in all of the small huddles of ladies who were eagerly reading the paper and the poem within it. His confidence bolstered, Andrew took his time as he wandered along the pathway, feeling a sense of pride and, indeed, a growing confidence within himself. Perhaps his work was more than satisfactory after all.

CHAPTER THREE

"You *must* have seen the poem! Everyone is speaking of it."

Charlotte shook her head, looking at Miss Marshall, somewhat amazed that her friend spoke with such awe over one small poem.

"My sister has told me of it, saying that it is only a few lines long, but that it holds a great deal of feeling."

"It is overwhelmed with feeling," Miss Marshall replied, putting one hand to her heart. "My goodness, it still overpowers my thoughts and senses whenever I think of it." Charlotte said nothing, looping her arm through her friend's arm. She and Miss Marshall had been acquainted for many years, given that their fathers' estates bordered each other, but Charlotte had never once heard her friend speak with such passion before. "I know that you will think me foolish, given that this is my second Season, and I have heard a great number of gentlemen read a great many sonnets before, but there is something about that poem that is so very intriguing and so very beautiful at the very same time."

"Why is it intriguing?"

"Because," Miss Marshall answered, as they slowly made their way towards Gunter's, where they hoped to purchase an ice, "there must be a purpose behind the poem. It holds so much feeling that it cannot be anything less than a declaration of love made by one gentleman to a lady."

Charlotte frowned.

"We cannot know that it is a gentleman."

Miss Marshall scoffed at this immediately.

"Yes, we can," she stated, firmly. "No ladies would be able to have their work printed in The London Chronicle, I am sure, and besides that, there is a way about it that tells me that it is from a gentleman's hand." About to protest, Charlotte caught the sharp glint in Miss Marshall's eye and chose instead to remain silent. "Should you like me to tell you the words?" Miss Marshall asked when Charlotte said nothing. "You may laugh, but I have it memorized."

Charlotte blinked but nodded.

"But of course," she agreed, quietly. "I should like to hear it, I think, given that it has taken hold of society with such strength!"

Miss Marshall smiled, stopped, and then closed her eyes, reciting the words in an almost reverent fashion. "*'In fields of gold, where wildflowers throng, love's gentle breeze whispers its song. As we walk, hand in hand, our embrace so sweet, our lips, our hearts, our lives, now meet. A love, a flame that burns so bright, will guide us through the dark of night. Our love, so strong, will forever shine, a love so pure, so true, so divine.'"*

A light smile danced across Charlotte's face as she listened to the poem spoken, admitting to herself that the words were sweetly written. Miss Marshall took a deep breath and then let it out slowly before opening her eyes, one eyebrow lifted in question.

"Yes, it was very good." Charlotte lifted her shoulders and then let them fall. "Though I have heard and read poems of its like before."

"But do you not think that there is something so beautiful about this one?" Miss Marshall protested, her eyes widening. "There is something about it which speaks to one's heart. I am sure that the words could not have come from anything other than a deep and unrelenting affection for the lady, whoever she is."

Charlotte smiled.

"Mayhap."

Her friend let out a sound of exasperation and then shook her head.

"It is impossible to affect your heart, it seems."

Laughing, Charlotte continued to walk along the pavement, taking Miss Marshall with her.

"My heart is touched by the tender words, of course," she admitted, seeing Miss Marshall still frowning, "but I cannot understand why it has grasped society's heart. There must be many gentlemen or ladies who write such words."

What she did not admit to her friend was that she had never really let herself dwell on what love was, nor what it might be like to experience it. Her father and mother had always thought of a practical match and thus, Charlotte had considered it a waste of time to permit herself such flowery thoughts.

"But this might be from a gentleman who cannot reach out to the lady he loves in any other way than this!" Miss Marshall cried, a clear understanding suddenly coming to Charlotte. "It is trying to understand the reason behind those words that drives the *beau monde* to such distraction – as it has my own heart also."

"I see." Charlotte tilted her head towards the bookshop. "Might you wish to step in here for a time? I am sure that I can find you an excellent book of poetry that might make your heart sing all the more loudly!"

Miss Marshall laughed and then nodded.

"I know very well that you desire *only* to go to the bookshop and not to the milliners or the like, so yes, we shall. Though we are still to make our way to Gunter's, are we not?"

Charlotte nodded and then stepped into the shop without hesitation, a bright smile spreading across her face. This was where she felt the greatest joy, the place where she felt as though she belonged, far from the rest of society and all of its requirements. Taking a deep breath, she drew in the smell that seemed to pervade the entire shop, her happiness growing steadily as Miss Marshall moved ahead of her, ready to peruse some of the novels near to hand.

Charlotte considered for a moment, then made her way to the other side of the shop, wandering down the long rows of books and searching specifically for any books of poetry that she might discover. She knew of a few authors and liked one or two specifically, but they often wrote about the beauty of nature, or about their love of their homeland. To find romantic poetry would not be difficult, but it was not something that Charlotte herself had read very often. Given that she had no experience of being in love, the idea had not come to her to read about it.

Moving around the corner to the end of the bookshelves, Charlotte paused and then picked up one book, smiling to herself as she opened it. William Blake was a name she already knew and, interested, she began to read the first page, only for something to knock into her, jarring the book from her hand.

"Oh!" Charlotte scrambled to pick it up, her eyes taking in the damage that the book had sustained from being thrown to the floor. "Oh, goodness. The spine is quite damaged."

She bent her head to study it a little better, her face flushing with concern.

"My sincere apologies."

Charlotte looked up, only for her heart to slam hard against her ribs, making her breath catch. This gentleman, whoever he was, had the most wonderful eyes, swirling with flecks of gold. His jaw was tight, however, no smile lingering on his face, but instead a slight furrowing of his eyebrows which made it appear as though he was displeased at seeing her.

"It is quite all right," she murmured, moving a step back from him. "I shall purchase this book and there will be no difficulty, I assure you. It was an accident, nothing more."

"No, *I* shall purchase it," he declared, taking the book from her, his fingers brushing hers as he did so. "It was my fault, and I have no concern in doing such a thing."

Charlotte blinked, a little surprised at his bold actions.

"There is no need, I assure you."

The gentleman said nothing, lowering his dark head to look at the book a little more clearly.

"A book of poetry, I see."

"Yes, it is," Charlotte answered, a gentle heat swirling within her as he lifted his gaze to hers, perhaps wondering what it was that she was so interested in. "I hear that there has been a poem printed in The London Chronicle which has captured the heart of many a young lady."

A hint of a smile tugged at the gentleman's lips.

"And you thought to go and find more poetry to read, having been inspired by it?"

Hesitating for a moment, Charlotte lifted her shoulders and then let them fall.

"In truth, while I think the poem has its worth, I am seeking out another book of poetry that I might share with my friend, to show her that there are many other writers of poetry also. She might find herself just as caught up by one of those other poems as she is with the one in the Chronicle."

The smile which had been held lightly to the gentleman's face soon faded.

"You mean to say that you think the poem which was in the London Chronicle to have no particular merit?"

Charlotte spread out her hands, a little confused about why the gentleman appeared a little upset at this.

"I have read many poems, Sir, and think that, while the one in the Chronicle is beautifully worded, there are others which are just as delicate in their choice of phrase. Indeed, there has been poetry written about almost every subject known to man, and those words inspire, regardless of what subject they speak about!"

"I see." The gentleman sniffed and then looked down at the book. "This book is solely romantic poetry, however."

"Yes, that is so. I confess that I have not read as much romantic poetry as I have other types of poetry, but I know that William Blake is an excellent poet and I have enjoyed his work previously."

The gentleman opened the book and read for a few minutes, nodding slowly.

"He does write well."

"Might you have come to the bookshop in order to secure your own book of poetry?" Charlotte asked, though the gentleman quickly lifted his head and snapped the book shut as she asked that question, a sharpness coming into his eyes which Charlotte could not understand. "Poetry may often be written *about* ladies, but it is not *only* ladies who read it."

"I am well aware of that." The gentleman's tone had changed completely, going from an amiable tone to one which was rather sharp. "I am not inclined to read poetry. I am not inclined to read anything, in fact. My time is filled with greater considerations."

She blinked.

"Then why are you in a bookshop?"

The gentleman looked back at her for a long moment as if he was trying to come up with an answer, only for a small, crinkling smile to twist up the side of his mouth.

"Ah, that is because I am seeking a quiet rendezvous," he said, speaking in a low voice now, which was almost a whisper as it raked up Charlotte's spine. "I do hope that you understand, Miss...?"

Charlotte recoiled from him, refusing to give him her name.

"My book, if you please?"

She snatched it from his fingers and, without another word, turned on her heel and hurried back towards Miss Marshall, her heart pounding furiously. There was no doubt in her mind about what that gentleman had meant. He was a rogue and nothing short of it, declaring quite openly that he was looking for a place where he might twine his arms about a lady's waist, might pull her close to him, and bend his head to kiss her lips. Her heart pounded as she heard a quiet chuckle coming from behind her, making her go hot all over. This was, no doubt, the very sort of gentleman that her mother had insisted she avoid and, therefore, she was not about to give him her name, nor ask for his!

"You have a book, yes?"

Miss Marshall smiled at Charlotte, only for her gaze to dart over Charlotte's shoulder, her eyes flaring wide.

"I was not with him," Charlotte murmured quietly, aware that her friend was now gazing at the gentleman, perhaps aware of who he was. "He came upon me suddenly and I dropped the book when he knocked into me. Though I have no qualms with that, given that I thought to buy it already."

"You spoke to him?" Miss Marshall whispered, only for the gentleman to come to stand directly beside them, his eyes alight with evident humor, the edge of his lip curving.

"I do believe that I said I would purchase this for you, my Lady," he said, holding out his hand for the book. "It was my fault and—"

"No, thank you." Charlotte forced a smile, her nerves taut. "I want to purchase it for myself. It is no trouble. Besides which, it was an accident."

"All the same."

The gentleman reached forward and made to pluck it from her hand as he had done before, but Charlotte moved back, avoiding him and, in one swift motion, turning towards the shopkeeper.

"Good afternoon. Might I purchase this, if you please?"

The shopkeeper was an older man who smiled warmly and set Charlotte at ease, only for that smile to fade as he looked to the gentleman who, to Charlotte's frustration, came to stand directly beside her.

"I shall be paying for this."

Irritated now at his insistence, Charlotte turned to the gentleman, her chin lifting.

"I have already stated that I have no desire for you to purchase this on my behalf. Why must you be so determined, when I have already said no?"

The gentleman grinned at her and, despite her protestations and her upset, Charlotte's heart beat wildly for a few moments as his full attention was placed upon her. Yes, she determined, this gentleman *was* a rogue for, in knowing what he had said to her previously about seeking a rendezvous, she could tell from his easy smile, the twinkle in his eye, and the way that he tilted his head and lifted his eyebrow, that he was nothing but a flirt.

"I know that young ladies such as yourself are often told that they must not accept gifts, especially from those that they are not acquainted with, but on this occasion I believe that it is merited."

"And I do not."

The gentleman's smile faded just a little.

"Goodness, I had not expected a young lady of quality to be so stubborn!"

Charlotte lifted her chin, her stomach knotting, though she forced herself to speak just as firmly as she could.

"And I did not expect a gentleman to be seeking out a rendezvous in the middle of a bookshop!" she exclaimed, her face burning hot as she heard the bookshop owner make a small sound in the back of his throat, though he continued to wrap her book in brown paper and did not look at her. "Nor did I expect a gentleman of the *ton* to refuse to accept the request of a young lady, but to insist upon having his own way! That, I think, is not in the least bit gentlemanly – especially since we are not yet acquainted. That is the worst of it, is it not? We ought to have been properly acquainted, correctly introduced, and instead, you have insisted upon speaking with me and forcing your intentions upon me without so much as a thought!"

This was more than Charlotte would normally have ever said in public, more than she would have ever stated aloud had she been in company, and yet, with *this* gentleman, she felt herself emboldened. Whether it was his manner, his arrogance or his clear flirtation, something about him made Charlotte want to stand up against him and make it perfectly clear to him that she was not about to be taken in by him... and that meant refusing to accept his offer of purchasing her book.

"My word, you are rather fiery, are you not?"

"No, she is not usually," Miss Marshall put in, coming to place herself directly between Charlotte and the gentleman. "Mayhap it is simply that *you* have brought that determination out in her character, good sir? Though to my eyes, it is not unfairly brought."

This made the gentleman's smile break apart completely, a scowl replacing it.

"I hardly think–"

"Might I complete my purchase?" Charlotte asked, taking out her pin money and speaking directly to the shopkeeper rather than listen to the gentleman any longer. "If you please."

"But of course, my Lady."

The shopkeeper named his price and Charlotte paid him directly, making certain that there was no opportunity for this gentleman to step in between them and press the money into the shopkeeper's hand.

"I thank you."

With a warm smile, Charlotte turned to take her leave, Miss Marshall beside her, though she did not say a single word to the gentleman. Pulling the door open, she stepped back to permit another lady to walk inside only to see the lady's eyes flare and a light smile spread across her face, her cheeks filling with color. Curious, she turned her head and watched for a few moments as the lady made her way towards the gentleman directly, one hand reaching out to greet him so that he might bow over it.

"His rendezvous, I expect," she murmured, darkly, only for the gentleman's eyes to catch hers. He was not smiling, his hazel eyes seeming to turn very dark indeed as he looked back at her. With a shake of her head, Charlotte turned away and made her way out of the shop directly, Miss Marshall following her. "Goodness, what a disagreeable fellow!" Charlotte exclaimed the moment the door closed. "I found myself very irritated indeed."

"I could tell," Miss Marshall returned, a slight lilt in her voice. "I do not think that I have ever heard you speak so boldly! Though I will not say that it was not justified."

Charlotte offered her friend a brief smile, feeling a little embarrassed that she *had* spoken with such strength.

"You do not think that I was rude?"

Miss Marshall shook her head.

"No, not in the least."

"Do you know who he is?" Charlotte saw her friend's gaze drift away. "I thought him a rogue, I confess. Are you acquainted with him?"

After a few moments, Miss Marshall nodded.

"Though I am not acquainted with him, I know of him. I believe that gentleman is Lord Kentmore – a Marquess *and* a rogue. You are quite right to think that he is inclined towards flirtation and the like, for that is precisely the sort of fellow he is! But the ladies of London are very fond of him, despite his reputation."

Charlotte shook her head.

"I suppose that is what makes him a rogue, does it not? He is handsome, he is flirtatious, and no doubt there will be many a lady eager for his attention, mayhap in the misguided hope that *they* will be the one to ensnare him into matrimony!"

Her friend laughed softly.

"Indeed, though I think that they must all surely understand that such an idea is foolishness. He has proven, over the last few Seasons, that he has no interest in marriage so why ladies would then draw themselves to him, I cannot understand."

I can.

The thought was a swift and unexpected one and Charlotte flushed hot, a little astonished that she should think such a thing. Lord Kentmore was clearly the very worst sort of gentleman, and certainly was someone she ought to avoid, just as her mother had insisted... so why, then, could she not remove the memory of his golden-green eyes, holding fast to hers?

"An ice, then?" Miss Marshall tilted her head and looked back at Charlotte curiously. "You do appear a little flushed. Are you all right?"

"It must still be the trace of irritation within me," Charlotte laughed, making her friend giggle. "Yes, an ice is just what I need. Anything to put Lord Kentmore and his ridiculous arrogance out of my mind!"

CHAPTER FOUR

There are others that are just as delicate.
Scowling to himself, Andrew threw back the door that led to his study and stormed into the room. For whatever reason, his encounter with that irritating young lady had made him more than a little out of sorts – indeed, he found himself angered at some of her words. He had been reveling in how much the *ton* had been delighting in his words, had been glad to know that so many ladies of the *ton* were discussing it, and even meditating upon it, only to hear dismissive words come to him instead.

"It should not matter what a mere Miss thinks," he told himself, coming around behind his desk, slamming one hand down upon the table. "Why should I find myself concerned about her response?"

Closing his eyes, he took in a long breath, trying to tell himself that he was being ridiculous but, still, the thoughts would not leave him. Over and over, he saw the lady turn her gaze from his, her expression one of consideration as she had informed him that other work was better than his, that she found herself delighting in the poetry of other men rather than thinking that his was on the same level as theirs. Why that irritated him, Andrew could not say, but yet, it was like a needle that continued to drive into his skin.

"This is foolishness!" Throwing up his hands, he pushed himself up from the table and moved to walk to the other side of the room, only for a knock at the door to break through his thoughts. "Yes?"

"Lord Glenfield has come to call, my Lord."

"Show him in." Andrew kept his gaze on the window as his friend came in, taking in a breath and attempting to push his frustration out of his expression before turning around. "Glenfield, good afternoon."

His friend frowned.

"Whatever is the matter?"

Andrew's expression crumpled.

"I thought that... nothing, that is to say. Nothing at all."

Lord Glenfield lifted an eyebrow.

Sighing, Andrew went to pour them both a brandy.

"I thought that I had been able to keep my expression free of all that I have been thinking," he said, by way of explanation. "Brandy?"

"Yes, if you please." Lord Glenfield took it from him with a nod of thanks. "I did not think that you would be at home this afternoon, given that you were meant to be meeting with Lady Sternford. I stopped by only on the chance you would have returned a little earlier than anticipated."

Andrew rolled his eyes.

"I did not spend much time with Lady Sternford, unfortunately."

"And why is that? Did she not appear?" Lord Glenfield frowned. "I thought she made it very plain to you that she would be glad of your company."

A wry smile tipped Andrew's lips.

"It seems that most people heard her say such a thing," he replied, as his friend chuckled. "She said it into my ear in such a loud voice that almost every other person in the room heard her! Yes, we arranged to meet in the bookshop and yes, she did arrive – but I must make it clear that I only intended to acquaint myself a little better with her, that is all. Nothing more."

Lord Glenfield snorted.

"Then why meet in such a private place? Why not walk with her through the park and further acquaint yourself that way?"

Andrew considered then shrugged, a small smile twisting the edge of his mouth.

"Mayhap I would not have been able to acquaint myself with her in the way I desired, should I have done that."

The bark of laughter from his friend made Andrew grin, his frustration over the other young lady fading from him.

"And did you *acquaint* yourself with her as you desired?" Lord Glenfield asked, just as Andrew's irritation returned swiftly. "I see that you are frowning hard, my friend. I presume that she was not as willing as you might have hoped?"

"Oh no, it was not that," Andrew returned, rolling his eyes. "It was more that I found myself unable to be present with her without any further company for, given what one young lady said in the presence of the bookshop keeper, the man seemed quite determined to reorder the books in whichever part of the shop I was in!" Lord Glenfield's lips quirked but Andrew only scowled, his frustration now burning through him again. "That young lady, whoever she was, took it into her head to say aloud what it was that I had said to her only a few minutes beforehand – and had I known that she was going to say something, I would never have *dreamed* of speaking so."

"Why did you say it?"

"Because," Andrew sighed, heavily, "I was irritated. I came upon her unexpectedly and she dropped a book she had been holding – a book of poetry, I might add. I told her that I would purchase it for her, given that it was a little damaged, but she refused."

His friend frowned.

"And that troubled you?"

"I did not want her to refuse, but it was more that she..." Sighing, Andrew threw back the rest of his brandy, suddenly feeling rather foolish. "She compared my poetry with other poems she preferred."

A light of understanding came into Lord Glenfield's eyes. "You took offense because she did not think well of your poem?"

Another sigh and a flush of embarrassment crept up Andrew's chest.

"I might have taken it a little too personally. I have been greatly appreciative of those in the *ton* who *have* valued my work, and to hear this young lady essentially saying that it was not in any way different from any other poem did irritate me somewhat."

His friend nodded.

"So you spoke foolishly about your intentions as regarded coming into the bookshop?"

"It was not foolish," Andrew protested quickly. "All I did was speak the truth, though I mayhap ought not to have been so clear about it."

"And thereafter, what did you do?"

Andrew flung up one hand, his empty glass in the other.

"Am I at confession?"

"What did you do to make the young lady speak about your intentions in such a clear way?"

Andrew closed his eyes.

"I followed after her, delighting silently in how my honesty had set her ill at ease–"

"Because she did not care for your poem."

"Exactly." Andrew let out a hiss of breath, realizing now just how childish and foolish he had been. "I insisted upon paying for the book and she turned around and spoke both harshly and directly, telling the shopkeeper what it was that I had come to do in his establishment."

"And, I presume, she did not let you purchase the book for her?" Lord Glenfield asked, his lips tugging into a wide smile, despite Andrew's mortification. "My dear friend, you did not behave well, I must say! Rogue you are, yes, but you have never been rude."

Andrew closed his eyes for a moment, wishing that the sense of mortification would pass.

"I am aware that I did not respond well, Glenfield. But the deed is done and now I find myself here, eager to write another poem in the sole hope that she might find *this* one to be better than the others."

His friend blinked.

"You would take her lack of interest in your work and use it to push you to write again?"

"I would write regardless," Andrew clarified, knowing he could be truthful with his friend, even if Lord Glenfield did not truly understand. The fellow had only written a few letters in his life thus far and had no interest in either writing or reading poetry. "It was your suggestion that I write to The London Chronicle and, given that this first poem has been so eagerly accepted, I feel it is almost my duty to provide them with another!"

His friend took a sip of his brandy, swirling the remainder of it in his glass.

"But her appreciation for poetry other than your own is your steering force?"

Andrew did not answer, a little surprised at the fire which had sprung up within his heart, ever since his conversation with the lady. Instead, he shrugged lightly and then turned away on the pretext of pouring more brandy.

"Might I ask what this young lady's name is?" his friend asked, coming over with him, his glass at the ready. "I think I must meet her, given the influence she has had upon you."

"There is no influence, only irritation," Andrew replied, pouring himself a good measure before doing the same for his friend. "And as for her name, I have very little idea."

Lord Glenfield's expression filled with surprise.

"You are not acquainted with her?"

"No, I am not."

"And you did not think to ask her at the time?"

Andrew shrugged.

"I am a rogue, am I not? What care I for propriety?"

With a chuckle, Lord Glenfield lifted his glass to his lips and took a sip.

"Then you will simply have to point her out to me so that I can do the proper thing and make certain that we are correctly introduced."

A slight frown pulled at Andrew's forehead.

"For what purpose?"

"Well, I am looking to make a match this Season, am I not?" his friend replied, as something heavy dropped into Andrew's stomach. "This young lady sounds tenacious and determined, and I do see the value in that." His eyebrow lifted. "Pretty?"

Thinking back to when he had first seen the lady, Andrew's lips pulled flat. He did not want to admit to his friend that yes, he had found the lady pretty but yet, there had been a hint of gold in her fair curls and her blue eyes had been very striking indeed.

"I suppose that I would say so."

"Capital! Then I look forward to being introduced to her," Lord Glenfield grinned, lifting his glass as though he were toasting Andrew. "Mayhap we shall see her again at the ball this evening."

"Mayhap we shall."

Andrew muttered the words, failing to find even the smallest amount of either interest or happiness in the idea. At least, he considered, as the conversation turned to other things, if she was at the ball, then he would know her name, and that was something, at least.

∽

"Do you see her?"

Andrew winced as Lord Glenfield hissed into his ear.

"My friend, please. You need not be so eager."

"Oh, but I am! I want very much to meet the young lady who has caused you so much frustration," came the reply, as both he and Andrew himself looked out across the ballroom. "My goodness, it is something of a crush here this evening, is it not?"

"Yes, I suppose it is." Andrew looked around but could not see the lady, choosing instead to turn his eyes to the small group of young ladies standing near them. "If I find her, I will inform you. Ah, good evening to you all!" Smiling broadly, he brought his attention to them, his heart lifting just a little as three of the five looked back at him with obvious recognition in their eyes, and the other two quickly dropped their gazes, though their cheeks were flushed. Andrew's grin grew wider. Those two young ladies he had already swept into his arms on one previous occasion, and, no doubt, they would be eager for more of the same, should he offer it to them. The other three, though he was acquainted with them, had not yet shown any interest as regarded his flirtations, but Andrew did not mind that. In time, he was sure that most, if not all, of them would become interested.

"A good evening to you also, Lord Kentmore," one Miss Hayter said, her eyes soft as she gazed back at him. "Are you dancing this evening? We must hope that this is why you have come to join our conversation."

"Oh, but of course I am!" Andrew exclaimed, extending his hand for her dance card, which Miss Hayter gave to him directly. "I have also come to see what it is that you are all discussing, for I am *terribly* nosy, you see."

He grinned at this, and the ladies laughed with him, the color growing steadily in the cheeks of some.

"Well, I do not mind informing you, though I am sure that you will already be aware of it," said another, glancing around at her friends. "We are speaking of the poem that was in the London Chronicle, and wondering if there will be another next week, given just how much we adored it!"

"Mayhap the gentleman who wrote it – for we presume it was a gentleman, though we do not know for certain – might be encouraged to write again, to write to his love, whoever she may be." Lady Margarete sighed almost plaintively, putting one hand to her heart. "I think it a most beautiful gesture of affection."

"I do not think that it *was* a gentleman who wrote it." Andrew's eyebrows shot up as Lady Tabitha, a young lady whom he had not yet caught with his attentions, smiled all around the group, evidently seeing or sensing their shock and surprise. "I think it is a young lady, writing the desires of her heart to the gentleman she adores," she continued, as the ladies looked at each other with some murmuring to their companions. "It does not say that it be gentlemen or lady now, does it? Why do we think that it is a gentleman? Could it not be that a young lady feels such a great affection that *she* has put it into words and then posted it to The London Chronicle? Mayhap this gentleman she cares for does not think or feel as she does and thus, she is determined to make certain that he knows of it by having it printed in the paper. Is that not a reasonable expectation?"

"No, I do not think so."

The words came out of Andrew's mouth before he could stop himself, seeing every eye turn to him and, flushing, he shrugged and tried to make light of his fervent remark.

"What I mean to say is that I am of the mind of everyone else," he said, quickly. "I think the phrasing and the like means that it comes from the mind of a gentleman, though I might very well be incorrect in that."

"There is no way to tell, I suppose," another young lady sighed, her lips curving gently. "I do hope that it is a gentleman, for I should very much like to try to guess which fellow it might be."

This made a few of the young ladies laugh softly, their eyes shining as they contemplated the idea – and Andrew's pride grew furiously. His chin lifted, his shoulders pulled back and he stood as tall as he could, reveling in all that they thought of his work.

And then, a face appeared just to his left and that delight soon faded.

"Oh, Miss Hawick, good evening! And to you also, Miss Hawick, Miss Marshall."

Andrew scowled as the three ladies came to join them, his spirits beginning to pull low.

"Might I ask if you are acquainted, Lord Kentmore, Lord Glenfield?" Lady Margarete asked, as Andrew forced himself to pull his face into an expression of nonchalance, looking at the lady he had seen earlier at the bookshop.

"No, we are not," he said quickly, lifting his chin a notch as the young lady looked back at him directly, showing not even the smallest hint of embarrassment. "Though I should *very* much like to be acquainted with three such beautiful ladies."

The young lady he already knew said nothing and did nothing, looking back at him as though she were a statue made of marble. Her friend beside her looked away, though the third lady let out a small exclamation of obvious joy, clasping her hands in front of her.

"I should *very* much like to become acquainted with a gentleman who speaks so kindly and sweetly," she said, her voice a little high-pitched as though she were truly caught up with excitement. "How very good of you to say such a generous thing about us, sir."

"You are quite welcome."

Andrew looked to Lady Margarete who, after a nod to the lady, turned back towards him.

"Lord Kentmore, Lord Glenfield, might I present Miss Lillian Hawick, Miss Charlotte Hawick, daughters to Viscount Morton, and Miss Sarah Marshall, daughter to Viscount Somerville."

Andrew bowed low, as did Lord Glenfield, finding himself rather delighted now to know the name of the lady.

"I am delighted to be introduced to all of you."

"Miss Hawick, Miss Marshall, Miss Hawick, might I present the Earl of Glenfield and the Marquess of Kentmore."

As Andrew rose from his bow, the three ladies dropped into their curtsies, though only one of them was smiling. Miss Marshall and Miss Charlotte Hawick were looking at each other, a knowing look in their eyes as they both turned their attention back towards himself and Lord Glenfield.

"I am delighted to meet all of you," he heard Lord Glenfield say, an eagerness in the man's voice that Andrew did not understand. "Now, do tell us, ladies, what you think of the poem in The London Chronicle? We are all just discussing it, wondering whether it be a gentlemen or lady who wrote it."

"Oh, but I think it must be a gentleman, for it is so beautifully written and has just a fervency within its words!" Miss Lillian Hawick exclaimed, speaking before the others had even a chance to say a word. "I do not think that I have ever read the like!"

Andrew let himself smile, only to see the way that the other Miss Hawick turned her head away and murmured something to Miss Marshall, who then nodded fervently.

"And you?" Lord Glenfield asked, directing his attention directly towards Miss Marshall. "Might you have an opinion?"

"Oh, I do indeed," Miss Marshall replied, her eyes

bright as she smiled back at him. "I first of all thought that it was truly wonderful, only for my dear friend here to bring me a book of poetry which I have spent some time this afternoon reading. I am not about to state that the poem in The London Chronicle was poorly written, only to say that I now understand that there is a vast array of such works written and I am eager to read as many of them as I can. Some are written with such passion, I can barely breathe!"

"Truly?" Lady Margarete's eyes flared, her interest evidently piqued. "I should very much like to read this book of poetry, if you would be so good as to share it with me? I confess that I have not read very much poetry, and I would very much like to do so."

"I would be glad to share it," Miss Marshall returned, making Andrew's stomach clench. Lady Margarete had spoken with delight about *his* work only a few moments ago and yet now, after hearing the recommendation from Miss Marshall – which had been influenced by Miss Hawick – she appeared to have almost forgotten it!

"I am quite certain that there will be another poem in The London Chronicle very soon," he said, interrupting the conversation and having all eyes turn towards him. "Mayhap then we shall discover whether it be lady or gentleman who writes it!" With a small nod, he made to take his leave, only for one of the young ladies to make a small exclamation.

"Lord Kentmore, were you not to dance with some of us?"

Andrew closed his eyes briefly, then forced a smile.

"Yes, of course. You are quite correct. I would be glad

to take a dance from any of you." Within a few seconds, Andrew found himself with five dance cards and, having already signed Miss Hayter's, handed that one directly to Lord Glenfield. "How delightful," he muttered, seeing his friend grin. "I am to have my entire evening taken up with dancing!"

The ladies giggled at this and, one at a time, Andrew passed the cards to Lord Glenfield who, thereafter, gave them back to the ladies.

"And what of you, Miss Marshall?"

Andrew looked at Lord Glenfield, surprised to hear him speak so directly to one young lady in particular.

"I see that neither yourself nor Miss Hawick have offered me your dance cards," Lord Glenfield continued, his eyebrows lifting. "Might it be that you have no desire to dance? If it is, then I would find that a great pity given that everyone here is eager to do so!"

Miss Marshall and Miss Hawick shared a look and then, with a small smile, Miss Marshall slipped her dance card from her wrist.

"How very kind, Lord Glenfield. Yes, I should be glad to dance with you."

Miss Hawick's gaze steadied itself on Lord Glenfield though, for whatever reason, Andrew could not take his eyes from her.

"As should I," she said, clearly, "though I am feeling a little fatigued this evening so I think only one dance will suffice."

Andrew's gut twisted and he grimaced, though quickly pulled that from his expression for fear that the other young ladies would see him do so. It was clear to him that Miss Hawick had no interest in being in his company, and certainly had no desire to dance with him. Lord Glenfield recognized it too, handing the card back to Miss Hawick at once though he smiled as he did so, which irritated Andrew all the more.

"What a capital evening this shall be!" Lord Glenfield declared as Andrew, bowing his head, finally managed to take a step away from the ladies, detaching himself from them. "I look forward to dancing with each and every one of you."

"As do I, of course."

Andrew nodded, turned, and released a long breath, closing his eyes in relief at no longer having to be in Miss Hawick's company.

"She does not like you in any way, does she?" Lord Glenfield laughed and slapped one hand on Andrew's shoulder. "Are you certain that she does not know that you are the one who wrote that poem?"

"Quite sure," Andrew stated, firmly, sending a sharp look in his friend's direction. "It seems that the impression she has of me is a very poor one."

"Indeed. Clearly, she is not at all inclined towards rogues," Lord Glenfield chuckled. "But that will not matter to you, since you have practically all of the ladies in society eager for your company! One lady disinterested cannot be a great concern, I am sure."

Andrew took a long breath, set his shoulders, and nodded.

"Quite," he agreed, firmly, telling himself that he was being ridiculous in allowing his frustrations about the young lady to rise once again.

"And you are going to write another poem for The London Chronicle, are you not?"

Resolve poured into Andrew's veins.

"Do stop saying such things here, where someone might overhear! But yes, I certainly am. And this time, it shall be longer than two verses," he declared, making Lord Glenfield's eyebrows lift in surprise. "And I shall make certain that there can be no question over whether it is a gentleman or a lady writing it."

"I see." Lord Glenfield chuckled quietly. "And which young lady shall be your muse this time?"

Andrew shrugged, brushing aside that question though, much to his astonishment, the only face that came to his mind was that of Miss Hawick. Much to his relief, Lord Glenfield began to talk of something else entirely, though, try as he might, Andrew could not remove the image of the lady from his mind and that was very troubling indeed.

CHAPTER FIVE

*M*iss Marshall chuckled as they walked arm in arm through the park.

"I think you made your point very clear when you refused to offer him your dance card last evening."

Charlotte laughed along with her friend, recalling how Lord Kentmore's expression had melted into a thinly concealed anger, his coldness towards her evident.

"I do not care what a rogue thinks of me," she declared. "I know that I am not to be in company with any rogue and–"

"Lord Kentmore is not a rogue!"

Glancing over her shoulder to where her sister walked alone – having refused to come into company with Charlotte and Miss Marshall – Charlotte resisted the desire to roll her eyes. "Yes, my dear sister, he is."

"How can you say such a thing?"

"Oh, it is well known," Miss Marshall put in, bringing a scowl to Lillian's face. "He is not someone that I should be glad to associate with."

Lillian sighed heavily and Charlotte shared a look with Miss Marshall, trying her best to hide her smile. Lillian had been somewhat exuberant when being introduced to the gentleman and had clearly found him more than a little delightful. She had berated Charlotte for not dancing with the gentleman when she had the chance, and Charlotte had chosen to remain silent on the subject. Now, however, Miss Marshall was doing the answering for her.

"Lord Kentmore is a Marquess, and they have high standing in society." Lillian sounded as though she was pouting. "I cannot imagine for a moment that a gentleman such as he would ever dream of behaving in an improper manner."

"And yet, he does," Miss Marshall said, firmly. "You may ask your friends, or mayhap even your Mama, for no doubt she has already heard his name spoken throughout London. Did you know that he was seen in the company of a very wealthy widow of late, pulling her into the shadows of the ballroom?"

Charlotte glanced at her friend, her eyebrows lifting.

"Indeed? During a ball?"

Miss Marshall shrugged lightly.

"He is a rogue, after all."

"Mayhap he can be reformed." Lillian's voice was quieter now, sounding rather resigned and disappointed. "Mayhap it only needs one young lady for him to fall quite in love and then, never turn from her again."

"My dear sister, you would be better finding a suitable gentleman who does not *need* to be reformed," Charlotte told her, glancing back over her shoulder. "The

Marquess may be handsome and charming, but his character is not at all desirable. You would not be happy on the arm of a gentleman who looked at every other lady aside from you, would you?"

A long, heavy sigh came from her sister by way of an answer, and Charlotte nodded to herself, believing that Lillian now accepted what she had been telling her.

"It is a great pity that he is a rogue, given that he is so highly titled," Miss Marshall said, a little more quietly so that Lillian could not overhear. "Though his friend, Lord Glenfield, was quite delightful, I must say. We lingered in conversation for some time, and I found him very amiable."

"As did I," Charlotte agreed, smiling. "We danced the country dance, and he was excellent both in conversation and in manner. I was surprised to find him so, I confess, given that he is good friends with Lord Kentmore. He informed me that they have been very closely acquainted for a long time."

"Just because one is a rogue does not mean that the other will be also, I suppose," Miss Marshall answered. "I do hope that he is a respectable sort. I did find myself a little intrigued by him, I confess."

Charlotte looked back at her in surprise, though she said nothing. Miss Marshall had never once mentioned a single gentleman in such warm tones before now, but after only one dance and one conversation with Lord Glenfield, it appeared that she was a little taken by him.

"Goodness, whatever is the meaning of this?"

Pulling herself out of her thoughts, Charlotte came to a stop as she, Miss Marshall, and Lillian looked at the small, gathered groups of both ladies and gentlemen. There were some respectable fellows standing to one side of the paths, however, holding out copies of something, and for whatever reason, ladies were rushing up to them, taking a copy, and then returning to their group.

"I do not know," Charlotte murmured, a light smile lifting the corners of her mouth. "Though it does seem to me that there is some great excitement."

A loud gasp came from Lillian and, after a moment, her sister grasped her arm, hard.

"It must be the next poem!"

Charlotte made to reply only for Lillian to let out a quiet squeal and hurry across to the men selling whatever it was they held.

"The poem?" Miss Marshall sounded confused for a moment. "Does she mean–"

"It must be The London Chronicle," Charlotte answered, linking her arm with Miss Marshall's again. "The second poem from whoever wrote the first one must be printed in this issue, given the amount of excitement here!"

Miss Marshall leaned into her for a moment as they continued their walk.

"Will you think ill of me if I admit that I am a little interested in seeing what the new poem says?"

Charlotte laughed.

"No, not in the least. My interest is piqued also, though not in the same way, mayhap. I should like to see if there is a name to the poem, or if the anonymous author has gone on to reveal themselves to the *ton*. Given the reaction of society, I would think that they might now be bold enough to declare themselves."

"Shall we go and purchase one, then?" With a nod, Charlotte walked alongside Miss Marshall – though not with any haste – and together, they collected a copy of The London Chronicle, with Miss Marshall paying the fellow for it. Unhooking her arm from her friend, Charlotte waited until her friend had found the page and watched her face as she read the poem. "It is certainly longer."

"Oh?" A little surprised at how interested she was in the poem, Charlotte tried to push her curiosity down a little. "In what way?"

"It has four verses," came the reply, "and each one is beautifully written, I must say."

"It is on the same theme?"

Miss Marshall lifted her head.

"It is about love, if that is what you mean." She dropped her head again to read, only to suck in a breath. "Goodness! There is no doubt now as to the author."

Charlotte moved closer at once, looking down at the paper as Miss Marshall pointed to the bottom of the poem.

"It has a name?"

"No, but it states that it is by an anonymous gentleman." Miss Marshall's eyes rounded just a little. "Clearly this person wants to make sure that everyone knows that it is *he* who has been writing these poems rather than a lady. Mayhap he heard society whispering about the confusion and wished to bring clarity."

"Mayhap he did," Charlotte agreed, refusing to let herself read the poem until Miss Marshall was ready.

It was a strange thing, she considered, finding herself very eager indeed to read it, but also battling within herself not to do so. She had thought the last poem very pretty, though she had not felt the same overwhelming excitement as others, nor had she had the great swell of emotion in response to the penned words. Mayhap it was because she was so well read... or, she considered, turning her head away, she had never permitted herself to imagine what it would be like to be in love. She had always been quieter in nature and studious in her character, choosing practicality where she could and thus, she had considered her marriage would be so too. A suitable match over a love match and, thus, Charlotte had never permitted herself to even imagine what a love match would feel like. Dare she open her heart to the possibility? Dare she read that poem and let herself *feel* more than she had ever done before?

"I think there is more passion here now." Lifting her head, Miss Marshall handed Charlotte the paper. "Should you like to read it?"

Charlotte took it from her friend.

"Yes, of course."

Taking a small breath, she set her shoulders and began to read.

'A SWEET MELODY *strums my heart,*
Echoes in the corridor of my soul.
A joyous symphony that can never depart

It binds my pain and makes me whole.

Love's song you sing to me alone,
  Your eyes hold fast to mine.
  And with each word, my love is sown
  My heart to yours entwined.

My very soul is clung to thee.
  Do not turn your eyes away from me,
  The thought, it tears my heart.
  We must endure a little while
  The pain of being apart.

To be so far and yet so bound,
  No threat will make me flee.
  I cannot forget what we have found,
  My whole self is one with thee.'

"Well?"

Charlotte lifted her head, considering.

"It does appear to me that this is written by a gentleman who is seeking to communicate with his love, does it not? Especially now that he has signed it!"

"It is hardly a signature," Charlotte replied, with a roll of her eyes. "It states simply that it is by an anonymous gentleman, that is all! I cannot think that makes it particularly clear as to who it is that has written it."

"All the same, it is better than it simply being written as anonymous," Miss Marshall answered, coming to the defense of the writer and making Charlotte smile. "I think this gentleman, whoever he is, has written to The London Chronicle purposefully so that his lady love – whom he is kept from, it seems – knows of his love and affection."

"Mayhap."

Miss Marshall took the paper from Charlotte again and read over it slowly.

"I think it is quite beautiful. The words that he speaks are words of devotion and affection."

"And of hope," Charlotte conceded, "though you are right, it appears that he is set apart from the lady."

Miss Marshall's eyebrows lifted.

"Then you think well of it?"

Charlotte shrugged lightly.

"It is a poem about love and the hope of continued affection," she said. "I cannot see that it is any worse or any better than any other poem I have read." She laughed as her friend sighed heavily. "But I do not know much about love, and I will admit that I do not often read much poetry on the subject so I cannot be the very best judge of it." She tilted her head and studied the poem again for a moment, as Miss Marshall held it in her hands. "To me, there is something a little lacking though I do not know what it is."

"Lacking?" Miss Marshall scoffed and shook her head. "My dear Charlotte, there is nothing lacking in this."

"You are probably quite correct," Charlotte

answered, with another smile. "I, however, feel as though it lacks a little passion, as if it is the imagining of the writer rather than a true circumstance."

Miss Marshall frowned.

"And by that, you mean to say that you do not believe his words to be genuine."

"They certainly do come across as though they are, of course."

"But you have said that you have no experience of reading such poetry and know very little about love. You have never been in love, have you?"

Charlotte shook her head, a little embarrassment coming into her chest as she saw Miss Marshall frown. Perhaps she had spoken a bit too boldly, a little too firmly, sounding arrogant rather than considered.

"I have not been."

"Nor have I." Miss Marshall's tone had softened now, her lips curved into a small smile. "But I do permit myself to imagine what it will be like. I long for a gentleman with a kind heart and a steady character to speak such words to me!" She tipped her head, looking back at Charlotte carefully. "Do not you?"

Charlotte hesitated.

"I–"

"Good afternoon, Miss Marshall, Miss Hawick! How delightful to see you in the park this fine afternoon."

Dropping quickly into a curtsey, Charlotte smiled at Lord Glenfield, though she saw that Lord Kentmore was slowly approaching also, his hands clasped behind his back and a slight pull of his lips downwards informing her that all was not well. Perhaps he did not want to be in her company, but was still eager to speak with Lord Glenfield and thus felt himself pulled in two directions.

"Might I take a turn about the grounds with you, Miss Marshall?" Lord Glenfield asked, making his interest in the lady very obvious indeed. "Your chaperone is—"

"My mother is a short distance behind us," Miss Marshall interrupted, her eagerness making itself very plain indeed. "Might you excuse me for a moment?"

"But of course!" Lord Glenfield beamed at the lady and then turned his attention to Charlotte. "I do hope that you will forgive me for desiring to steal Miss Marshall from your company for a time, Miss Hawick."

Charlotte smiled back at him, finding him to be a very amiable sort, not at all surprised that Miss Marshall had taken to him so quickly.

"I quite understand. Miss Marshall is a very dear friend of mine, and I think very highly of her. I am sure that you will find the same."

Lord Glenfield nodded, perhaps hearing the slight hint of warning in Charlotte's voice.

"I am certain that I shall. I – oh, there you are, Lord Kentmore. I did not see you there."

"I have come to talk with you, as you asked." Lord Kentmore's tone was a little sharp, his eyes darting towards Charlotte's for a moment, though he inclined his head towards her just as he ought. "Good afternoon, Miss Hawick. Forgive me for interrupting your conversation. It is only that Lord Glenfield and I were to be talking about various things which is precisely why I came to the park in the first place."

Charlotte, a little surprised by his rude manner, lifted her chin.

"I shall not delay your conversation any longer, Lord Kentmore. Do excuse me."

"Please, there is no need," Lord Glenfield exclaimed, quickly. "I am to walk with Miss Marshall, and I am sure that Lord Kentmore would be glad to take a turn with you also."

With a shake of her head, Charlotte looked to Lord Kentmore who was slowly beginning to turn a strange shade of red.

"It is not necessary," she said, though she forced a smile to her face so that Lord Glenfield would not think her rude. "I think I shall return to my mother for the time being, and permit Miss Marshall to walk with you without my company." She inclined her head, then turned on her heel and walked back towards her mother, passing Miss Marshall as she went. The bright, beaming smile on Miss Marshall's face and the light which shone in her eyes was quite at odds with what Charlotte herself felt and, recognizing that her irritation with Lord Kentmore grew all the more. Why did he have to be so unpleasant? Why were his words so harsh, his tone so disinterested? He was meant to be a rogue, a tease, a flirt – so why, then, did he appear to be so at odds with her?

CHAPTER SIX

Andrew gave himself a slight shake as he stepped into the ballroom, determined to put all thought of Miss Hawick from his mind. He could not understand what it was about her that pressed her into his thoughts with such persistence but, try as he might, he could not forget about her entirely. It was as though she had some sort of hold on him, a hold he could not get her to remove. He had watched as Miss Marshall had come back to walk alongside Lord Glenfield, delight in her expression and, he had noted, a copy of The London Chronicle in her hand. How much he had wanted to ask her what she thought of the poem within it! And more than that, how much he had desired to find out what Miss Hawick had thought of it also!

"Which is foolishness," he told himself, stoutly. "I have no reason to think about her, especially when I have a great many other ladies of the *ton* interested in my company!"

With a nod to himself, he took a deep breath and

then strode into the room, lifting his head and smiling as some of the ladies in the room glanced towards him. It had been some days since he had last made an alliance, had last caught a young lady about the waist and tugged her into his arms, and that was a little frustrating, given that the reason he was failing in that particular way was solely due to Miss Hawick.

"Good evening, Lord Kentmore. How very good to have you join us this evening. Are you to dance, I wonder?"

Andrew grinned, taking the hand of Lady Faustine and greeting not only her but the three other ladies in the group, all of whom he was already acquainted with.

"How wonderful to be in your company again, my Lady," he said, for this was the first time he had been in the company of the lady since the previous Season. "I do think I shall dance this evening, yes. Why? Might you be willing to step out with me?"

The lady's eyes glittered.

"I may have to rest," she sighed, a little plaintively. "Much to my relief, however, Lady Southend has opened one of her private parlors for me so I can go there whenever I require."

"I quite understand." Andrew released her hand but kept his smile pinned, knowing full well what it was that she was suggesting to him. "You must rest whenever it is that you require it."

The lady tilted her head gently.

"It may be that I will dance and, thereafter, be required to sit down and rest," she suggested, as Andrew's interest quickened, understanding precisely what it was that she required from him.

"Of course. And is there a desire to dance with me, Lady Faustine? I would be glad to take you to the parlor thereafter, if it was necessary." Lady Faustine's eyes flashed with warning and Andrew looked away, suddenly a little embarrassed by his own fervency. He had made himself much too obvious while in company. "Though, of course, if you wish only to dance one or two dances this evening, I shall not take offense."

"I am grateful for your understanding," came the reply with what looked like relief coming over Lady Faustine's expression. "I will not be able to accept your offer, however, though I am sure that my dear friends would be glad to stand up with you. It was for them that I asked in the first place, you understand."

Andrew smiled and turned his attention to the other three ladies, all of whom were smiling warmly back at him.

"But of course. Goodness, fortune smiles favorably upon me this evening, does it not, to be able to dance with three such beautiful ladies?"

He threw a quick glance to Lady Faustine, seeing the smile on her face fade just a little though, when he offered her a barely perceptible nod, it returned with its full glory. As he took in the three dance cards, however, Andrew's attention snagged on something... or someone. With a start, he saw that not only was Miss Hawick gazing at him steadily, but that she was standing close enough to hear everything that he had been saying to Lady Faustine. Andrew narrowed his eyes just a fraction as if telling her that he was not about to be cowed by her stare and her clear dislike of what he was choosing to do, but Miss Hawick did not relent. Instead, she tilted her head up and kept her gaze steady, her lips thin and her eyes sharp.

It was Andrew who looked away first, recalling how quickly she had removed herself from his company, how eager she had been to step away from him instead of taking a turn about the park alongside Lord Glenfield and Miss Marshall. That should not be niggling away at him as it did and, much to his dismay, simply seeing her again made him recall that all the more clearly.

He scowled.

"Is everything quite all right, Lord Kentmore? You have not yet signed the dance cards."

Andrew looked back at Lady Anna, smiling quickly.

"Indeed, all is well. The only thing that troubles me is how I am to decide which dance I am to take for all of you and, indeed, being disappointed that I can only take the one!"

This brought a bright smile back to Lady Anna's face, and when Andrew dared a glance towards Miss Hawick again, she was no longer looking at him. Telling himself to forget about her entirely, Andrew returned his attention to the ladies before him and smiled warmly at Lady Faustine, knowing precisely what was waiting for him later that evening.

Much to his dismay, however, as he made his excuses and made his way back around the ballroom again in search of yet more company, his interest in Lady Faustine and his anticipation of the warm embrace she would offer him slowly began to fade. Indeed, it faded so quickly that it was as though something had punctured it, making it dissipate in only a matter of seconds. Scowling, Andrew rubbed one hand down his face and turned instead to watch the couples dancing the polka.

This is all Miss Hawick's doing, he told himself, sternly. *I need to set her aside, forget about her entirely, and thereafter, do all that I can to return to the life of the unrepentant rogue.*

~

She still has not come.

Andrew let out a long breath and continued to pace up and down the parlor floor. Lady Faustine had, in a rather loud voice, informed her companion that she was soon to dance with Lord Dalton and, thereafter, would find herself required to go and rest, given that she was so very fatigued that evening. Andrew, fully aware that she had those words so that he would hear them, had quickly made his way to the parlor in expectation of her arrival. That had been some time ago, however, and as yet, she had not appeared.

Scowling, Andrew rubbed one hand over his face and then made his way to the door. This evening had begun badly, with his thoughts of Miss Hawick lingering in his mind, only for him to then see her practically glaring at him as though she had any right whatsoever to judge his actions! Now, however, it appeared to have become much worse, since Lady Faustine had either chosen *not* to come to meet him, as she had made so plain, or had, mayhap, forgotten about the arrangement. It was not as though he was the only one that she spent time with - that he knew all too well – but, in the past, that had suited him, given that he had no interest in furthering his attachment to her either. At the moment, however, it felt as though he had been punched hard in the stomach, with the air thrown out of him, his chest tight and blood hissing in his ears. Pulling open the door, Andrew strode out into the dark hallway, a short distance from the ballroom, only for a gentle exclamation to meet his ears.

Relief flooded him.

"There you are," he growled softly, wrapping his arms around Lady Faustine and lowering his head so that his forehead touched hers. "And here I was, thinking that you had abandoned me!" Without hesitating, without even thinking about pulling her into the parlor, Andrew lowered his head and kissed her fiercely, a little surprised at the reluctance he felt there. It was not as though Lady Faustine was pushing him away, only that she appeared to be a little... limp. Her arms had not gone around his neck, he had not felt her lean into him, had not had her tilt her head to deepen their kiss. Frowning, Andrew broke the kiss and lifted his head, hearing the gasp come from her and struggling to understand what the concern was.

"Charlotte? I think we have come the wrong way. I – oh, good gracious!"

Charlotte?

Andrew stepped back at once, shaking his hands as though he had touched something unpleasant and now sought to rid all trace of it from himself.

"I – I beg your pardon, I–"

"Whatever were you doing to my sister?"

In the dark hallway, Andrew could not make out the face of the lady who was speaking. Nor, much to his frustration, could he see the face of the lady he had held in his arms. His mind clung to the name, telling him that he did know who it was but, in his struggle, in his confusion and upset, he could not recall it.

"It was nothing short of a mistake, I assure you. You must forgive me." A sudden realization of what might take place, should either one of these ladies demand that he make this situation right, slammed hard into his chest and he caught his breath, fear twisting in his heart. "Please, forgive me. I will take my leave of you now and–"

"I hardly think so!" The second lady strode forward, though the first caught her and held her back. "This is disgraceful!"

"It was a mistake, Lillian," said the first lady, her voice barely loud enough for Andrew to hear. "Come, we should return to the ball. I–"

"Just who are you?" the second voice demanded and, much to Andrew's horror, she picked up one of the nearby candlesticks and brought it close to him – and he could do nothing but permit her to see his face. "Oh, goodness!" The lady's eyes went wide before she turned her head back. "Charlotte, it is Lord Kentmore!"

A slightly strangled sound echoed towards Andrew, and he closed his eyes, his heart hammering.

"As I have said, this was nothing but a mistake. I can do nothing else other than beg your forgiveness. Please, permit me to take my leave so that nothing more occurs."

The second lady placed one hand flat on Andrew's chest as he began to move away.

"Do not think for a single moment that I will let you walk away from my sister after what I witnessed," she hissed, though there was a glint in her eye that Andrew did not much like. "My sister's reputation is utterly ruined, and you will do as you ought, Lord Kentmore." Andrew squeezed his eyes closed, his whole body turning to fire. This was utterly dreadful. He was now expected to betrothe himself to this young lady, to *marry* her, which was the very worst situation imaginable! *Why did I not wait to make certain it was Lady Faustine? Why was I so hasty?* "Well?"

"Lillian, please."

"Charlotte, you must be silent." The authority of the second young lady rang about the hallway and despite his desire to escape, despite his desire to run from her, and to free himself from the situation, Andrew knew he had no other choice but to accept it. Thanks to his own idiocy, he was now to become betrothed to this young lady. His future looked very black indeed. "Lord Kentmore?"

"Very well," Andrew hissed, squeezing his eyes closed and hating every word that came from him. "If I must, then I will betrothe myself to... well, to whoever you are."

"You mean, you do not know?" The young lady in front of him laughed, her hand falling from his chest. "My dear Lord Kentmore, you are now courting – for I do not think it would be fair to betrothe yourself immediately without questions being asked." She cleared her throat. "As I was saying, you are now courting my sister, Miss Charlotte Hawick."

It was as though the entire building had fallen, crushing him. Andrew struggled to breathe, staring at the young lady opposite him, still not quite able to make out her face. The very young lady he had been struggling not to think of, the one who irritated him, the one who clearly disliked him, *she* was the one he was now tied to?

"And you will betroth yourself to her very soon, else all of the *ton* shall know of what you have done," Lillian Hawick stated, firmly. "Now, do excuse me, Lord Kentmore, as I take my sister to go and speak with our father. He will have to know all, and I am sure that he will wish to speak with you also, very soon."

She strode off without a word, putting one arm around her sister's shoulders and making to pull her away.

Charlotte Hawick did not move.

"I – I do not want this."

Her sister let out a snort.

"Whether you want it or not, this is what must happen." Her voice echoed back towards Andrew as she led Charlotte away, seemingly working through her sister's reluctance. "You are going to be the Marchioness of Kentmore, Charlotte! What could be better than that?"

Andrew closed his eyes again, his shoulders rounding as he realized the reason that Miss Lillian Hawick had demanded such a thing. To have a Viscount's daughter betrothed to a Marquess was significant indeed, and would improve the family's standing in society a great deal, which, in turn, meant that Lillian herself would be more likely to make a match with a higher titled gentleman. Groaning, he sucked in air, his mind whirling, his heart aching, just as a sob echoed down the corridor towards him.

What have I done?

CHAPTER SEVEN

"I must say, I do so much enjoy dancing." Charlotte tried to smile, knowing that she would be entirely unable to reply to Lord Templeton, given that she was being forced to concentrate on the dance. When he had first asked her for her dance card, he had not been in his cups nor had he shown any inclination towards imbibing, given that he had refused to take a glass when it had been offered to him. Now, however, he had clearly drunk a little too much whisky and was flailing a little, his steps narrowly missing her feet on occasion, and his hands slipping much too quickly from hers. "You are quite beautiful, I must say, though a little too quiet for my liking," Lord Templeton continued, grabbing her around the waist, his hand tightening there painfully. "I do hope that you are happy dancing with me? After all, I am one of the most sought-after gentlemen here in London."

"Of course."

It was all Charlotte could say, and she was relieved

when his hand fell from her waist as they separated again. Praying silently that the orchestra would not play for too much longer, she gritted her teeth and continued on with the dance, vowing never to dance with Lord Templeton again.

"Alas, our dance must come to an end!"

Lord Templeton grabbed her hand and made to bow over it as the music slowed, only for him to lean a little too far forward, lose his balance, and plunge forward. With a gasp, Charlotte side-stepped him quickly, pulling her hand away just as he careered past her, only for something to rip.

Her eyes closed, mortification creeping up over her as she saw others looking at her, perhaps aware of what had just taken place.

"Charlotte, do walk with me." Without warning, Lillian took her arm and led her from the floor, her head held high and a light smile on her face. Charlotte, certain that her face was very red indeed, struggled to project the same confidence. "I saw what Lord Templeton did," Lillian murmured, out of the corner of her mouth. "Are you all right?"

Charlotte, touched by her sister's concern, nodded.

"I am, though my gown is torn at the hem."

"There are bound to be maids ready to assist us," Lillian answered, determinedly. "Goodness, Charlotte, what a thing to have happen!"

Looking at her sister as Lillian stopped briefly to inform their mother of what had happened and what they now intended to do, Charlotte felt her heart warm, despite the embarrassment. This was the first time in a long time that Lillian had shown her such consideration, and Charlotte appreciated it a great deal. After reassuring her mother that she was not injured, Charlotte followed Lillian, hoping that very few of the *ton* would notice her ripped gown.

"You are very kind to be so considerate," Charlotte said, as they stepped out into the hallway. "Had you not come to take me away, I am sure that I would have been broken with mortification!"

"You are my sister, Charlotte," came the reply, as Lillian turned to the left, walking down one of the hallways which, Charlotte thought, did not look particularly well lit. "I care for you. Besides which, you do not often dance, and I did not want you to be discouraged from stepping out again, simply because of the foolishness of one gentleman! It is good for me *and* for you, that you should be seen dancing."

Charlotte's smile was a little rueful as she understood the reasons for her sister's sympathy and support. Yes, she *did* care for Charlotte's situation, and did not want her to be embarrassed but, at the same time, saw the advantage in having Charlotte dancing. It would detract from the view that society might otherwise have of her as being quiet and reserved which, in turn, might encourage the gentlemen of London to consider them both with interest.

"I am not certain that this is the right way," Lillian murmured, coming to a stop. "Mama told me that there was a room just down the hallway and–"

"She might have been speaking of the *other* hallway," Charlotte pointed out, quite certain that the dark hallway with only one or two candles was not where they were meant to go. "Might you go to look, Lillian? I do not want to make my way there for nothing, for fear that someone will see the state of my gown."

Her sister nodded.

"Of course. If I find the parlor where the maids are, I will come to fetch you. It might be best if you remain here for a few minutes. I will be as quick as I can be."

"Thank you, Lillian."

Smiling, Charlotte watched her sister hurry away, finding her spirits lifting as she did so. Lillian was so very different in nature to her and yet, despite that, there was still a bond between them; a bond which Charlotte did not always feel, or even sense but, during moments like this, it was a comfort. Turning back to the hallway, she began to meander slowly along it, straying not too far from where Lillian had left her. The music and laughter from the ballroom still echoed towards her, but Charlotte slowly grew to appreciate the quietness surrounding her. She still did not particularly enjoy balls and the like, and though Lillian was eager for her to dance again, inwardly, Charlotte knew that she would prefer to stay back from it all.

A slight frown darted across her forehead as she recalled seeing – and hearing – Lord Kentmore's conversation with one lady whom Charlotte had not been acquainted with. She had not overheard everything that he had been saying, but the parts she had overheard simply by standing near him, had been very flirtatious indeed. It was quite clear to Charlotte that Lord Kentmore and that lady had been hopeful of some kind of encounter, and that Lord Kentmore was eager to facilitate it. She had found her stomach tightening, her heart thumping hard against her chest as she had overheard them, and was a little surprised at the flush of jealousy that had rushed through her. She had quickly broken apart that reaction into tiny pieces and thrown it aside, refusing to let it linger, and finding that she felt nothing but disgust at the notion. She did not want to have Lord Kentmore's interest pushed towards her! And nor did she want him to consider her with any sort of interest. As far as she was concerned, that gentleman was nothing but someone to be avoided.

Just as that thought came and went, the door near where she was standing opened and a figure stepped out. Charlotte's breath caught in her throat, and she made to back away, only for strong arms to grasp her tightly, hauling her against a very solid figure indeed.

Suddenly, she couldn't breathe.

"There you are! And here I was thinking that you had abandoned me."

Charlotte opened her mouth to say that she had no knowledge of what he meant, trying to ask him to remove his hands from her, only for his head to descend and his lips to press against hers.

At that moment, everything shifted. It felt as though the ground was no longer solid beneath her feet, and her heart was pounding furiously as a wonderful sense of heat and fire burned through her. She was helpless against him, her need to step away vanishing into smoke as he held her tight, his embrace filling her with a sense of such astonishment and delight that she did not ever want it to fade.

"Charlotte? I think that we have come the wrong way. I – oh, good gracious!"

Lillian's voice seemed to come from very far away, though the moment that her voice broke through the empty space, the gentleman dropped his hands and backed away as though he had burned himself. Charlotte, dizzy and blinking furiously, looked at him, trying to make out his face, but the shadows kept that from her. Heat filled her all over again but, this time, it came from a sense of shame that she had ever let herself be so foolish as to let a gentleman – a stranger, no doubt – kiss her!

"I – I beg your pardon," the gentleman stammered, his voice sounding vaguely familiar. "I–"

"Whatever were you doing to my sister?" Lillian rushed close to Charlotte, one hand going around her shoulders. Charlotte shook her head wordlessly, wanting her sister to say nothing more, to draw back rather than push forward. The words stuck in her throat, her mortification binding her lips closed as she battled a sudden surge of tears. Whatever had she been thinking?

"It was nothing short of a mistake, I assure you. You must forgive me." A slight pause followed, only for the gentleman to speak again, his voice more fervent this time. "Please, forgive me. I will take my leave of you now and–"

"I hardly think so!" Lillan began to stride forward but Charlotte reached out and caught her arm, trying to pull her back. "This is disgraceful!"

Charlotte's heart pounded.

"It was a mistake, Lillian." Her heart slammed hard against her ribs, fear beginning to take hold of her now. This matter could be easily dealt with, she considered. She did not know who this gentleman was and, no doubt, he did not know who *she* truly was, given the darkness of the hallway. All she needed to do was leave and the matter would be at an end. "Come, we should return to the ball. I–"

Lillian pulled her arm away.

"Just who are you?" Free from Charlotte's grasp, Lillian walked across to the other side of the hallway, picked up one of the nearby candlesticks, and brought it close to the gentleman in question. Charlotte closed her eyes, hearing her sister's exclamation. There was no escaping this now. Lillian had taken the decision from her, it seemed, determined to discover who this fellow was, despite Charlotte's urge to return to the ballroom. Silence filled the hallway for a moment and, despite her uncertainty, Charlotte's heart pulled apart with two equally strong desires – the desire to know who this gentleman was, who had kissed her with such passion, and the desire to set it all aside and return to the ballroom, pretending that nothing had happened. "Charlotte, it is Lord Kentmore!"

Unable to prevent a strangled exclamation breaking from her lips, Charlotte took a step backward, one hand to her heart. *Lord Kentmore?* Her mind began to whirl, dizziness coursing through her as she swallowed hard, her other hand going to her lips. Lord Kentmore, the rogue, the scoundrel, had been the one to kiss her? There was nothing worse than this, she considered, nothing more dreadful than learning that it had been he who had clasped her in his arms.

"As I have said, this was nothing but a mistake. I can do nothing else other than beg your forgiveness. Please, permit me to take my leave so that nothing more occurs."

Lord Kentmore's voice was filled with a desperation that Charlotte could well understand, and she forced herself to step forward, trying to take hold of her sister before she could do any more.

Again, Lillian was more determined than she was.

"Do not think for a single moment that I will let you walk away from my sister after what I just witnessed. My sister's reputation is utterly ruined, and you will do as you ought, Lord Kentmore."

No. Tears welled up in Charlotte's eyes, seeing what Lillian meant and shrinking back from it.

"Lillian, wait."

Her voice was only a whisper, making no impact upon her stubborn sister.

"Well?"

Lillian's singular word was directed at Lord Kentmore. Charlotte took a breath.

"Lillian, please."

Instantly, Lillian waved one hand in Charlotte's direction, barely turning to glance at her.

"Charlotte, you must be silent." Her voice echoed back towards her, holding a greater strength than Charlotte had ever imagined her sister would possess. "Lord Kentmore?"

There came another moment of silence, only for the gentleman's voice to break through.

"Very well."

No, I cannot!

The threatening tears fell to Charlotte's cheeks, her strength gone from her as her shoulders rounded, her head falling low. Deep down, she knew that Lillian was quite right to do as she was doing, but all the same, Charlotte wished that she had not said a word. No one had seen them, no other person from society had witnessed them in that embrace, had they?

Not that you know of, at least, said a quiet voice in her mind. *What if someone has seen you and is now waiting to see who will emerge from the hallway, ready to whisper it through the ton? Then what will you do?*

"If I must, then I will betrothe myself to... well, to whoever you are."

"You mean, you do not know?" The laughter that came from Lillian clashed hard against Charlotte's despair and confusion. "My dear Lord Kentmore, you are now courting – for I do not think it would be possible to betrothe yourself immediately without questions being asked." She cleared her throat. "As I was saying, you are now courting my sister, Miss Charlotte Hawick." *He did not even know it was I.* Charlotte closed her eyes and released a slow, calming breath, though it did nothing to quieten the frantic beating of her heart. Through all of this, Lord Kentmore had not known for a moment that it was she whom he had been kissing and was now betrothed to. For a moment, she wondered what his reaction was. She was still unable to make out his features but was quite certain that it would be just as she felt – dismay, dread, and darkness. "And you will betrothe yourself to her very soon, else all of the *ton* shall know of what you have done," Lillian stated, her voice and stance speaking of nothing other than sheer determination, forcing Lord Kentmore and Charlotte into this situation though, Charlotte had to admit, there was wisdom in what her sister was insisting upon. "Now, do excuse me, Lord Kentmore, as I take my sister to go and speak with our father. He will have to know all, and I am sure that he will wish to speak with you, very soon."

Charlotte did not move, watching as Lillian turned on her heel and came back directly towards her. Lillian smiled gently, her eyes shining with a strange light that Charlotte could not quite understand.

"Come, Charlotte." Putting one arm around Charlotte's shoulders, she made to turn her around, made to walk her away from Lord Kentmore, but Charlotte remained fixed to where she stood, her whole body suddenly hot and filled with a dreadful fear. Yes, she knew that this was what should be expected of a gentleman who had done such a thing – albeit without recognizing that it was she he had been kissing, and not the lady he had expected – but the realization that she would soon be his wife, the wife of the dreadful rogue who was the Marquess of Kentmore, made her heart shudder.

"I – I do not want this."

Lillian shook her head, letting out a snort as her hand fell from Charlotte's shoulder, only instead to grasp her wrist.

"My dear sister, whether you want it or not, this is what must happen. You are going to be the Marchioness of Kentmore, Charlotte! What could be better than that?"

"The thought is a dreadful one to me," Charlotte whispered, staggering slightly as Lillian forcibly pulled at her wrist and tugged her away. "Lord Kentmore is a rogue, Lillian! He was, no doubt, expecting someone else to join him - and this is the gentleman that you wish me to accept?"

"It is not *I* who wishes you to accept him," Lillian answered, as they made their way back down the hallway. "It is because you must, that is all. The *ton* will expect it."

Charlotte shook her head, a slight weakness coming into her frame as her sister led her back towards the ballroom.

"No one from the *ton* is aware of it, Lillian!"

"You cannot be sure of that." Her sister stopped suddenly, turning to face Charlotte and releasing her wrist. "Charlotte, this is an excellent match, if only you would see it. You are to be a Marchioness! That means that your standing will be increased dramatically, that your wealth and—"

"None of that matters to me." Charlotte closed her eyes briefly, putting one hand to her forehead, her whole body feeling fatigued and heavy. "Tell me, Lillian, that you did not insist upon this simply because of the hope that your own standing would be improved?" She opened her eyes, but her sister said nothing, looking back at Charlotte with a slight wariness in her expression. "Lillian." Charlotte's voice grew hoarse. "I cannot do this simply because you want to improve your standing and your chances of finding a higher titled gentleman to wed you."

"That is one of the benefits of what must take place, I will admit that," Lillian answered, with a sniff, "but I have insisted upon it because, as you well know, it is what must be done. You cannot pretend that all is well, Charlotte! The gentleman kissed you! I saw you, yes, but there is no certainty that there was no one else present. What if the lady he was *meant* to be with appeared and saw the same thing, perhaps listening in the shadows for your name? What then?"

A shiver ran down Charlotte's spine.

"I – I do not think that would be very likely."

"But you cannot say for certain." Charlotte shook her head, wordlessly. "Then it still stands," Lillain answered, firmly. "Now, we will go to have your gown repaired and then–"

"I am going to go home."

Lillian blinked at her.

"What?"

"I must retire. There is too much for me to think about, too much for me to consider, for me to simply return to the ballroom and pretend all is well." Charlotte's voice was thick with tears, her heart aching terribly. "You might very well be delighted at all of this, Lillian, but I am not. Instead, I am broken-hearted."

Her sister frowned, clearly having very little understanding as to what it was that Charlotte felt.

"I will take the carriage and then have it return here," Charlotte continued, turning away from her sister, praying that she would make it to the carriage without a single tear falling. "Tell Mama that I have a headache or some such thing. Pray, do not tell them anything of Lord Kentmore. I will do so myself, when tomorrow comes."

There were no words of comfort, no gentle understanding or sympathy from her sister in response to this. Instead, with a shrug, Lillian turned away and made her way back to the ballroom. Charlotte, her eyes stinging, went quickly to the door of the house, asking one of the footmen to find her carriage. As she stood there in the dark, her arms wrapped around herself, Charlotte closed her eyes and dropped her head, no longer able to hold back her tears. Her entire world had shattered in one moment, and her shame and mortification burnt so hot that it felt as though it would slice right through her. Had she not given in to the kiss, had she not lost herself in delight and wonder, then none of this would have happened. She would have disentangled herself from Lord Kentmore's embrace long before Lillian had appeared and would, thereafter, have been kept quite free of him. She would not now find herself practically betrothed to the fellow, would not have her future set and determined.

All was now black and broken before her and yet, it was a path that Charlotte had no choice but to walk.

CHAPTER EIGHT

*A*ndrew rubbed one hand over his face, scowled, and slammed one fist down hard on the table.

Try as he might, he could not see a way to escape this. He had stayed up almost all night, thinking about a way to remove himself from Miss Hawick, a way to say that he was no longer going to court her, nor betrothe himself to her, but the more he thought of it, the more difficult it became. Time and again, his thoughts would return to what he had seen of her as she had stood at the door of the house, waiting for her carriage.

His heart had twisted and, even now, whenever it came to mind, it did the very same again.

She had not known that he had been there, of course, else he was sure that she would never have let herself be so free in her emotions. No doubt she would have stood there, resolute, until she had finally climbed into her carriage and left him behind. She had not, however, and Andrew had been able to see the full extent of her upset. She had crumpled into herself, her arms wrapping around her waist as though she were trying to seek out some sort of comfort, her head dropping forward and quiet, tiny sobs breaking from her lips. Andrew had no doubt that she had been crying, finding himself imagining the tears on her cheeks, the salt on her lips... and all because of him.

That had been – and still was – a painful truth to accept. His foolishness had been the reason for all of this, his determination to enjoy an assignation with Lady Faustine had become his one and only focus, to the point that he had lost all sense. He ought to have made certain that it *was* the lady in question who had come towards him, ought to have spoken her name at least before pulling her into his arms. Instead, he had acted on instinct and with desire, letting that pull him forward rather than choosing sense. The pain that he had obviously caused Miss Hawick cut deep into his soul, making him flood with guilt and frustration, mortified that he had behaved in such a way and, at the same time, angry with himself for what he would now have to endure.

A knock came at the door and Andrew growled for the butler to enter, only for Lord Glenfield to make his way into the room. His eyebrows lifted as he took in Andrew's expression, though he said nothing, simply walking across the room to pour them both a measure of brandy.

"It is almost time for you to step out into society again," he said, after settling himself into an overstuffed chair to the side of Andrew's desk. "The soiree this evening, yes? Lord Bannington's?"

"Yes, yes, I recall."

His friend tilted his head.

"You left the ball very early last evening, without any sort of explanation. Are you quite all right?"

Andrew considered his answer, wondering whether he should tell his friend all, only to realize that Lord Glenfield would discover the truth, whether it was spoken now or not. Heaving a sigh, he closed his eyes and leaned back in his chair.

"Last evening, I found myself betrothed to Miss Hawick." The silence was telling, and Andrew opened his eyes to see that his friend's mouth had fallen open, a glaze coming into his eyes as he stared at Andrew in utter shock. "I know, I know. It was not something that I planned, as I am sure you can understand."

"You... you are betrothed?"

Andrew sighed again, waving one hand vaguely.

"I must court her for a short time, so that the *ton* do not suspect that there has been something improper occur, but yes, I am to be betrothed very soon. Within a fortnight, I expect." Lord Glenfield blinked quickly and then threw back his brandy in two gulps before staring at Andrew again. "And yes, before you ask, it was entirely my own fault. The reason I left the ball and returned to the house was so that I might try to find a way to escape this betrothal but, as yet, I have come up with very little."

"How..." Lord Glenfield closed his eyes. "I must ask how such a thing is possible! How can it be that you are betrothed to a young lady? Andrew shook his head wordlessly, feeling shame bite down hard at him as he tried to find the words to explain. "You did something foolish, I presume?"

Nodding, Andrew swallowed hard and looked away, finding it difficult to explain to his friend what had happened without feeling overwhelmed with mortification.

"I thought she was Lady Faustine."

"Oh."

Closing his eyes, Andrew let out yet another sigh.

"Believing that, I captured her in my arms, only to be discovered by Miss Lillian Hawick, her sister, who then insisted that I do the honorable thing and betrothe myself to her sister."

Lord Glenfield nodded slowly.

"Which is quite right," he agreed, as Andrew scowled. "You cannot damage a lady's reputation in that way and expect nothing to come of it."

"Though, had she stepped back, had she pushed me away or fought me, then I would have known that I had made a mistake, and nothing would have come of it!" Andrew exclaimed, slamming his fist down on the table again. "I–"

"You are not about to blame the young lady herself for this, I hope?"

Lord Glenfield's voice had taken on a darker tone and, embarrassed, Andrew dropped his head and shook it.

"No, I suppose that I should not."

"You most certainly should not!" Lord Glenfield exclaimed, getting up to pour himself another brandy. "You did not see that it was not Lady Faustine?"

Andrew shook his head.

"It was dark and I, being a little frustrated that she

had not arrived – Lady Faustine, that is – stepped out of the room to return to the ballroom, only to see the figure of a lady approaching."

"Whom you then assumed was Lady Faustine."

"Yes."

Lord Glenfield nodded slowly, meandering back towards his chair.

"You left the ballroom a little early, simply because you wanted to escape the difficulty you faced? Because you did not want to go to speak to Lord Morton, you decided to return home, and see if you could find a way to break the connection between yourself and Miss Hawick?"

Shrugging, Andrew looked away again, hearing the hint of disappointment in his friend's voice.

"I am a rogue, after all. I do not want to take responsibility for this, I do not want to marry her."

"That matters not. All that matters is that you *are* to wed her," his friend told him, unequivocally. "You cannot escape from this, not after what you have done. So might I suggest that you prepare yourself, come to the soiree and, if Lord Morton is there, speak to him directly."

Letting out a low groan, Andrew pinched the bridge of his nose, waiting for the wave of frustration to fade away.

"I do not want to do any of that."

His friend snorted.

"You shall, though."

With another groan, Andrew lifted his brandy to his lips and took a sip, waiting for it to improve his spirits but, instead, it only sank them lower. His shoulders dropped, his jaw tightening as he forced himself to relinquish all hope of ever being free of this, of being free of *her*.

"I suppose that there is every chance that Viscount Morton will refuse me. That must give me some hope, at least."

His friend snorted.

"Very little hope, I am afraid. You are aware that you are a Marquess and she, the daughter of a Viscount? Why ever would a gentleman of that standing refuse a gentleman of *your* standing?"

Andrew scowled and pushed himself to rise.

"Then I shall remind myself that, should he accept my request to court Miss Hawick, nothing really needs to change. I can continue on just as I am, albeit with a little more discretion." He grinned at Lord Glenfield, expecting his friend to laugh and smile in response but Lord Glenfield only frowned, not even the smallest hint of laughter on his face.

"You would continue to pursue other ladies, even though you have a wife?" he asked, as Andrew considered the question, aware of the tug of conscience in his mind, aware that there was a slight flicker of guilt in his heart even at considering it.

"I can see no reason not to." His friend's eyebrows lifted. "There are many married gentlemen who are just as they have always been," Andrew protested, hearing his words but feeling them to be a little weak. "I did not choose this. I did not choose *her*! So therefore, I cannot see why–"

"I will pray that such a view will change, in time," his friend shot back, a little quickly. "Now, are you to attend the soiree or not?" He cast a sharp glance towards Andrew. "For if you are, you will have to change."

Andrew glanced down at his shirt, seeing the crumpled lines and the slight stains from where he had splashed his brandy earlier in the afternoon. It was a very good reason *not* to attend, he told himself, for he could simply state that he was not at all prepared and had no desire to go, and all would be well.

But then I should be a coward, he reminded himself, scowling. *I know what I must do and hiding here will not remove the need to do it.*

"Yes, I shall attend," he muttered, a little unwilling still. "If you wish to depart without me, I shall find you there once I arrive."

A small hint of a smile danced about Lord Glenfield's lips.

"Then I shall wait, I think."

"Oh?"

His friend laughed and sat back in his chair, stretching out his legs in front of him and crossing them at the ankle.

"Why, it is to make certain that you are not going to turn around and decide *not* to attend after all," he said, making Andrew grimace. "I should not like you to change your mind, you see, so I think I shall wait until you are quite ready so that we might depart together, as we intended."

There was nothing for Andrew to do but walk out of his study and make his way to his bed-chamber, ringing for his valet the moment he arrived. His thoughts and considerations had come to nothing, and were *worth* nothing. At the end of it all, he was still tied to Miss Hawick, still forced into a position that he had never desired to be in, but now could not escape from.

I will have to marry her, he thought to himself, scowling. *My life, as I know it, has come completely to an end – and it is all my own fault.*

～

"Good evening." Andrew inclined his head to his host, mumbled a thank you to him for the invitation, and then made his way a little further into the room, just as he usually did. There was no confidence about him this time, however, no sense of expectancy that he would find some wonderful connections present this evening, and might have some enjoyment of his own with them. Instead, he felt himself a little fearful and, hating that sensation, scowled hard and lifted his chin, setting his shoulders straight as he looked about the room.

"She is not here as yet, though she and her family have accepted the invitations to attend," said a voice in his ear as Andrew glanced back at his friend, seeing Lord Glenfield smile. "Yes, you may wonder how I discovered this, but know that it was through speaking quietly to one of the footmen. Now," he continued, "you need to stop looking so fearful. It is quite clear to me that you are concerned about what will be said and done this evening, but worrying about it is of no purpose."

Andrew snorted.

"That is easy enough for you to say, my friend. You are not the one who must seek out the lady's father and beg for her hand, even when you do not truly wish to do so."

His friend shrugged.

"I am afraid that you will not find me with any sympathy. I think you foolish for what you did, and the consequences are quite fair, though I do hope that the young lady herself is quite contented with it."

Andrew's jaw tightened as the memory of seeing Miss Hawick in tears threw itself back at him.

"Miss Hawick is not at all delighted with our betrothal. Her sister is, however."

"Her sister?"

Andrew nodded.

"It was she who determined that I had to become betrothed to Miss Charlotte Hawick. I do believe that Miss Charlotte would have been more than contented to step away from me, to leave things just as they were."

"As you would have been also."

Andrew nodded.

"Precisely." Again, the image of the lady crying as she waited for her carriage hit him and he licked his lips. "However, thanks to Miss Lillian Hawick's insistence, I now must court the lady. I must consider betrothal and matrimony."

"It may be that she cares for her sister and wants what is best for her," Lord Glenfield replied, a little gently. "I know that you are upset, and frustrated that this has all come about, but I can see the purpose in Miss Lillian's actions." His gaze went over Andrew's shoulder. "Ah, I can see that they have now all arrived."

"They have?" Andrew spun around, only to turn

back again just as swiftly as he caught Miss Charlotte Hawick's eye. "Goodness, so she has." His heart slammed hard into his chest. "And I am going to have to go and speak with her father very soon."

"No doubt either the lady herself, or her sister, has spoken to him on your behalf already," his friend remarked, tilting his head just a little. "I must say, Miss Lillian Hawick is rather pretty this evening, is she not?"

Groaning, Andrew closed his eyes.

"Please, do not make such remarks as that! I am well aware that Miss Hawick – both of the Misses Hawick, in fact – are very pretty, but that does not make me feel any better. I think–"

"Do excuse me, will you?"

Andrew blinked in surprise, his eyes following his friend as Lord Glenfield made his way directly towards Miss Lillian Hawick, taking her aside from her mother and speaking warmly to her, making the lady smile. Andrew did not know what to think, utterly astonished that not only had Lord Glenfield found Miss Lillian Hawick pretty enough to go and speak with directly, but that he had also willingly abandoned Andrew, apparently without so much as a thought! It was as though Andrew's present circumstances were not of any real consideration and that, in itself, frustrated Andrew more than a little.

His stomach clenching, Andrew made his way directly towards Lord Morton, his chin lifting as he fought to steady both his gaze and his heart. It was clamoring furiously, knowing that with these next few words, he would be determining his future without any ability to step aside.

"Lord Morton." Andrew cleared his throat as he bowed his head, tension rippling through him. "I am afraid we have not been introduced but–"

"You must be Lord Kentmore!" Much to Andrew's surprise, the gentleman beamed at him as though he were some long-lost friend and, thereafter, clapped Andrew on the shoulder. "You are the gentleman who is interested in courting Charlotte, I believe?"

Still rather stunned, it took Andrew a few moments to answer, his throat rasping as he nodded.

"Yes, that is so."

"Capital! I know that we have not been formally introduced, but I do not believe that it is needed," the gentleman said, grasping Andrew's hand and shaking it firmly. "My daughter has told me all about you, telling me that I need not fear your reputation, for you are quite determined to turn your back upon all of that now. To think that a gentleman such as yourself would find yourself so caught up with Charlotte is quite remarkable, I must say!" He finally released Andrew's hand, his eyes still bright and his smile wide. "Of course you have my consent, Lord Kentmore! I could think of nothing better for Charlotte, I assure you."

A small wave of guilt rose up in Andrew's soul, only to break down over him.

"I am not quite certain that I am the very best sort of gentleman," he said, surprised at how much feeling rose up within him as he spoke, as though to rebel against what he knew to be the truth. "But I shall do my best as regards Miss Hawick."

The gentleman's smile – which had never faded – grew larger still.

"I am certain you shall. My goodness, what a delight this is to me! To know that you have been quite captured by the beauty and the nature of *my* daughter is quite remarkable, I must say, especially given that she can be so very quiet and reserved."

"What is that I hear?"

A voice that Andrew did not recognize came from behind him and, glancing over his shoulder, he saw a lady coming to stand beside Miss Charlotte Hawick and Lady Morton.

"Oh, it is just that the Marquess of Kentmore has sought out my husband's permission to court Charlotte," Lady Morton answered, as the other lady gasped in evident surprise. "My husband has given his consent, so now Lord Kentmore shall be courting my daughter! Is that not wonderful?"

"It is indeed!" the other lady replied, pressing Lady Morton's arm before turning and, as Andrew watched, scurrying across the room to spread the news.

His heart sank. Yes, he knew that this was what had been expected of him, what he'd had no choice but to do, but all the same, the reluctance within him grew steadily. He did not want to become betrothed to Miss Hawick, did not want to spend every day with her by his side. All he wanted was to free himself from her, but now, with the news spreading through the room, that seemed nothing but impossible.

"You will wish to spend time with her this evening, I am sure."

Andrew turned back to give his attention to Lord Morton, who was still beaming at him, his whole face wreathed in smiles.

"Spend time with Miss Hawick?"

"Yes," Lord Morton answered, a slight dimming of his smile following. "I presume that you—"

Andrew cleared his throat.

"Yes, yes of course." Forcing a smile, he turned to the lady who was still standing by her mother, her face a little pale. "Miss Hawick," he began, hating every word that came out of his mouth. "Might you wish to take a turn about the room?"

Miss Hawick closed her eyes, a slight tremble about her lips.

"No, I do not think that it would be proper to do so."

The answer made Andrew recoil, taking a slight step back as he regarded the lady. He had not expected her to refuse him, had thought that she would see that there was nothing for them to do but to accept what was now before them, and to act as it required.

Her mother, clearly a little shocked, blinked quickly, then trilled a laugh.

"My dear, you must not think that there is any sort of concern here about propriety or the like! So long as you do not leave the room, you are permitted to walk with Lord Kentmore for a time, without a chaperone."

Miss Hawick looked to her mother as though she were desperately trying to get her to read her thoughts, but Lady Morton merely lifted an eyebrow. With a small sigh, and not even the smallest, flickering smile on her face, Miss Hawick stepped forward and looked up at him.

Her eyes were red-rimmed, and a heavy weight dropped into Andrew's stomach.

"Very well, Lord Kentmore," she said, her voice dull. "A walk around the room it shall be."

Andrew offered her his arm without saying anything further but, much to his surprise, the moment she took it, he was filled with a flush of heat, as though he were secretly delighted to have her so near him. That in itself was foolishness, he told himself and, as they walked away from Lord and Lady Morton, Andrew's heart began to sink all the lower. There was naught but tension, strain, and upset here, and he had not even a single hope that there would ever be any sort of happiness between them. Not today, not tomorrow, and certainly not in their future.

CHAPTER NINE

"Miss Hawick, your father wishes to see you in the study."

Charlotte, who had been attempting to read, looked up at once.

"My father?" She had not seen him since the previous day and, given that she had barely slept, only to then fall asleep at the time the maids rose to start the day, Charlotte had not been very present with any of her family. Part of her had hoped that her sister would forget about the entire situation, that Lord Kentmore would not move forward with his responsibilities, and that all would be well. Thus, she had tried to put the whole thing out of her mind, had determined that she would speak to Lillian whenever she saw her next and to beg her not to speak to their parents about what had taken place.

Now, however, she feared that Lillian had done more than she ought.

"Did he say what it was about?"

The footman shook his head and then stepped to one

side, holding the door open for Charlotte to exit the room. Charlotte knew as well as the footman that she could not keep her father waiting and thus, feeling herself all of a tremble, she rose and made her way from the room. Her heart pounded furiously, her hands clenching and unclenching as she walked to the study, only to find the door open and the sounds of voices coming from within.

"I did not know that he even was acquainted with her!" she heard her mother say, fear beginning to climb up her throat, making her want to scream aloud, to refute all that Lillian had clearly told them. "I must say, this is something of an astonishment."

"Thank you for telling us, Lillian. It is no surprise that your sister did not wish to, given that she is a good deal quieter and more reserved than you are. I am sure that she will be very grateful."

Grateful? A sudden twist of anger tore through Charlotte, and she made her way into the room directly, her eyes flashing to her sister who, seeing her come in, quickly looked away.

"Charlotte! Thank you for coming. Your sister has informed us of a conversation which took place last evening while she was present." Her mother came closer to her, a bright smile on her face. "The Marquess of Kentmore seeks to court you?"

Charlotte lifted her chin.

"Mama, the Marquess of Kentmore is a rogue."

"Yes, but for you, I am certain that he will change his ways," Lillian interrupted, ignoring the sharp look that Charlotte threw at her, unspeakingly demanding that she remain silent. "He expressed himself so warmly last evening, I am quite certain that he will not remain a rogue for long."

"I did not want you to speak of this to our parents, Lillian," Charlotte said, sharply. "I believe that I told you last evening that *I* would speak to them about it."

Lillian pouted.

"I was only being a considerate sister," she responded, a slight glint in her eye which Charlotte was quite certain her mother and father did not see. "You are much too shy about such things, and I am sure that you have already convinced yourself that such a request was not made in earnest! Thus, you are now likely determined to keep it to yourself, and Lord Kentmore's desire would never have been made known, and you would have missed out on a wonderful match!"

"Wonderful?" Charlotte could not keep the derision from her voice, her hands on her hips as tears sparked in her eyes. "Lord Kentmore is a scoundrel! I have no promise that he will change, despite what you say."

"And yet, we must consider it," Lady Morton answered, softly. "My dear girl, this is, as your sister has said, an excellent match. I understand that you might be concerned as regards Lord Kentmore's character but—"

"You warned both myself and Lillian to stay away from such gentlemen!" Charlotte exclaimed, tears now falling down her cheeks. "But now you wish me to marry one? That does not make sense, Mama. How can I do such a thing?"

Lord Morton harrumphed quietly, though it was enough to bring a stillness to Charlotte, a recognition that her father's authority was over her still. She closed her eyes and inclined her head, pulling out her handkerchief to dry her tears.

"I confess that I do not fully understand your tears, though I must agree with both your mother and your sister. To be matched with a Marquess, whatever his reputation, is an excellent match for the daughter of a Viscount, and I do not think that you should let it pass by." Charlotte squeezed her eyes shut all the more tightly, fighting to keep the tears from falling like rain. "I find myself quite delighted with it if I am to be honest," her father continued, his happiness sounding in his voice. "My daughter shall be a Marchioness! This will bring our family's standing all the higher, which is excellent indeed!"

Charlotte choked back a sob, hearing Lillian's words repeated in her head alongside their father's. It was clear to her that her father considered social standing of great importance, just as Lillian did, and now, evidently, there was to be no stepping back from this. Charlotte would have to marry Lord Kentmore regardless of her feelings.

"Then it is decided, yes?" Lady Morton threw a smile to her husband who returned it with a nod of his head, leaving Charlotte standing alone, feeling utterly dejected. "No doubt he will come to speak with you this evening, Morton, if he is in attendance at the soiree."

"I shall be delighted to meet him!" came the enthusiastic reply, as Charlotte turned to make her way from the room. "A remarkable circumstance, truly remarkable. To think that our youngest daughter would make such a superb match, my dear!"

Charlotte walked out of her father's study, hearing

the three of them still discussing her courtship and connection to Lord Kentmore while, at the same time, seeming not to realize that she had taken her leave of them. Thanks to Lillian, the situation had been revealed to her parents and their enthusiasm seemed to know no bounds. No one had asked her how she truly felt. Yes, they had listened, but they had not taken it in, had not given her concerns any credence. Instead, they had simply thought of their own standing, the improvements that her connection would bring, and had set her aside entirely.

Finally reaching the solace of her room, Charlotte sank onto her bed, pulled out her handkerchief, and burst into tears.

She had never felt so alone in all her life, and there was not a soul present to comfort her.

∽

There he is.

Charlotte's whole body jolted as Lord Kentmore caught her gaze, though it was not all entirely from upset. She had to admit that Lord Kentmore did look handsome tonight, though that was not something she had previously been unaware of. There was little doubt that he was a handsome fellow, given just how easily he could capture the attention of many a young lady within the *ton*. She, however, was not about to be affected.

"I do hope you know that I have done this for your best," Lillian murmured, just as Lord Kentmore glanced back at her again. "You may not like it, but you know that it is the right thing to do... for everyone." Charlotte said nothing, choosing not to confide in her sister any longer. She had been touched by Lillian's concern for her at the ball with her ripped gown but what had happened thereafter had caused Charlotte to be entirely distrusting now. "And now you will not speak to me?" Lillian let out a snort as Lord Kentmore and Lord Glenfield looked towards them again. "There is nothing that could have been done, Charlotte. You know that."

"You could have remained silent, as could have I," Charlotte countered, speaking so quietly so as not to have her mother overhear them.

"And what if someone from the *ton* had seen you?"

"Then I could have waited to see if that was a possibility," Charlotte answered, sharply. "I know that this was not something which I thought of at the time, but upon considering the matter, I think that–"

"Miss Hawick, Miss Hawick." Charlotte was forced to stop as Lord Glenfield came to them, a broad smile on his face as he inclined his head. "A good evening to you both. I wonder, Miss Hawick, if I might draw you into conversation for a moment?"

Lillian, ever ready with her enthusiasm, let out a small exclamation and then stepped away from Charlotte and their mother almost at once, though they did not go far.

"But of course, Lord Glenfield. Now, tell me. Has Lord Kentmore told you about the present circumstances?"

Charlotte closed her eyes in mortification, wishing that she could find a shadowy corner in which to hide herself. Her sister was much too enthusiastic – and much too forward – for Charlotte's liking, and it brought her nothing but embarrassment. Opening her eyes, Charlotte's breath hitched as she saw that Lord Kentmore had come to speak with her father and was doing so already, glancing over his shoulder to her once or twice. Her stomach dipped, her fears burning hot trails down her arms and legs, only for Lord Kentmore to turn to face her, a small smile on his lips which did not ignite any sort of spark in his eyes.

"Miss Hawick." He inclined his head. "Might you wish to take a turn about the room?"

Charlotte closed her eyes, sensing the slight tremble about her lips as she fought to keep her whirling emotions under tight control. No, she wanted to say, she had no interest in walking with him, had no desire to spend even the smallest amount of time in his company. Her entire world had been shrouded in darkness ever since he had kissed her, and he was the one responsible for it. Scouring her mind to find an answer, to give him an excuse as to why she could not possibly be in his company, she lifted her chin a notch.

"No, I do not think that it would be proper to do so."

Instantly, Lord Kentmore took a small step backward, astonishment filling his expression – astonishment which then quickly turned into a grimace. Evidently, he had not been expecting her to refuse him.

A laugh came from her mother, however, as her hand went to Charlotte's arm.

"My dear, you must not think that there is any sort of concern here about propriety or the like! So long as you do not leave the room, you are permitted to walk with Lord Kentmore for a time without a chaperone."

Please understand how uncomfortable this makes me, Mama, Charlotte thought to herself, looking long at her mother only for Lady Morton to lift an eyebrow at her instead. Charlotte's heart twisted, a sigh breaking from her lips as she realized that she was not to have any sort of escape.

"Very well, Lord Kentmore," she said, hearing the sorrow in her voice, but doing nothing to hide it. "A walk around the room it shall be."

Her mother smiled her acceptance of this and, having no choice but to place a hand on his arm, Charlotte let herself be taken away from the safety of her mother's company, being led around the side of the room by Lord Kentmore.

They said nothing. The silence between them grew thick and Charlotte's mind clouded, her shoulders dropping as they continued about the room. Lord Kentmore cleared his throat once, twice and then took a long breath, turning to look at her.

"Miss Hawick, I suppose that I should, first of all, apologize for what I did."

"Apologize?" Charlotte glanced at him, aware of the sharpness of her tone. "Tell me, do you seek to apologize for what you did because of the consequences it has brought, or because of the action itself?"

Lord Kentmore swallowed but held her gaze.

"I thought you were someone else so yes, I apologize for the action I took, given that it was not you who was meant to be in my arms."

A sudden shiver ran through Charlotte's frame as her eyes drifted to his mouth, the memory of what it had been like to be held so tightly and kissed so passionately reverberating through her. And then, she shuddered, recalling the sort of gentleman he was and what she could expect from him as her husband.

"No doubt you will tell me that it is not something you intend to turn from?"

"Turn from?"

Charlotte looked at him again, her breath quickening a little as she fought to find the words.

"I – I mean to say that you will continue to be a rogue even though we are soon to be betrothed and married?"

She felt a tightness in her chest, her heart squeezing painfully as she saw a flicker of light coming into his eyes, only to fade away.

"I will not promise that I shall never return to such a way of life," he said, candidly. "But for the time being, during our courtship, betrothal, and marriage – and wedding trip – I shall do nothing other than devote myself to you." A wry laugh broke from his lips. "Lord Glenfield tells me that he believes things might change between us, that I might find myself suddenly very contented indeed, but I am not entirely convinced."

Charlotte said nothing for some moments, a faint flicker of hope igniting itself in her heart. Lord Kentmore might be the most dreadful rogue at present, but he had committed himself to her for the time being, which was something, was it not? And what if, as Lord Kentmore had suggested, things changed within his heart so that he *wanted* none but her?

"You must tell me some things about yourself, Miss Hawick," Lord Kentmore continued, changing the subject entirely. "If we are to court and soon become betrothed, then it is right that I, as your intended, know as much about you as I can."

A little surprised, Charlotte looked away.

"You already know that I do not tolerate foolishness and flirtation, Lord Kentmore," she said, tightly. "And that I enjoy reading. Is that not enough?"

A small sound came from Lord Kentmore's throat.

"Yes, I well recall that you read a great deal of poetry," he said, sounding irritated - as though, somehow, her answer to his question had been a cause of frustration in some way. "You are, I think, the only young lady in London who does not find herself affected by the poems in The London Chronicle, given how many *other* poems you have read which you can measure it against."

Feeling a little attacked, Charlotte rose to defend herself.

"I am well-read, and I do not consider that a bad thing," she retorted. "To me, the gentleman who writes the poetry in The London Chronicle lacks a little passion. There is also the fact that, in the last poem he wrote, all but one of the lines rhymed, which makes me wonder if he is truly *feeling* what he writes, or if it is simply a matter of stating what he can to garner as much feeling from others as possible."

"You give your opinion very assuredly for someone who is a little reserved."

She looked at him.

"I do. I know what I speak of, and I will not pretend otherwise to satisfy the ego of any gentleman."

This made Lord Kentmore blink rapidly, evidently astonished that she would think to speak as boldly to him as she had done. Charlotte said nothing further, however, though inwardly she felt a small curl of satisfaction that she had rendered him practically silent. She was not ashamed to state that she knew poetry well, for it was something that she read very often, as she had done for many years. Lord Kentmore, she considered, certainly would not have the same expertise, given that he, no doubt, had not spent many hours scrutinizing each word, reading each line, and wondering at the meaning. No, Charlotte thought to herself, a hint of a smile on her lips now, she could have perfect confidence in this... and Lord Kentmore was not about to take that from her.

"Are you not going to ask me anything about myself, as I have asked you?"

A little surprised, Charlotte looked at him again.

"What is there that you think I need to consider?"

She resisted the desire to point out to him that, though he *had* asked her a question, he had not garnered any further knowledge from it, given that she had simply reminded him of things he already knew.

"You know nothing about me."

A broken laugh came from her lips, though she shook her head at him thereafter, the edge of her lip curling.

"Lord Kentmore, I believe that I know as much about you as I need to."

His jaw tightened.

"I hardly think so."

"You are a rogue. A scoundrel, who enjoys nothing more than spending all of his time garnering as much attention from society ladies as he can," Charlotte returned, quickly. "Your hobbies are, I expect, shooting, riding your horse, and playing cards – and, no doubt, gambling with it. Thereafter, while you are in society, you want to do nothing other than flirt, tease, and embrace whichever lady your eyes fall upon, and whichever one of them stirs your interest, you *must* have in your arms for a time – for none of them are permitted to enter your heart! You do not think of any other aside from yourself, you do not let yourself be swayed by the concerns or even the interests of others. Instead, you turn away and keep your eyes fixed solely upon yourself. There is arrogance and selfishness within you, and you do not care." She turned to face him, her hand still on his arm but pulling away from him slowly. "Is there anything that I have said which is incorrect, Lord Kentmore? Or is there anything more that I should know of you that I do not already?" A shadow passed over Lord Kentmore's expression, his jaw flexing as his hazel eyes searched hers. He opened his mouth, let out a huff of breath, and then closed it again, shaking his head as if to say that he had decided not to speak at all. "And this is the gentleman I am to marry."

Charlotte closed her eyes, the words coming out as a whisper, though she had not meant to speak them aloud. A tightness came into her chest, tears burning in her eyes and though she fought them, though she tried her utmost not to let a single tear fall, she could not prevent it. As she opened her eyes, one dashed to her cheek and though she caught it, sniffed and blinked furiously to keep the rest back, she feared that someone had seen it fall.

An expression passed over Lord Kentmore's face, something that Charlotte could not make out. He frowned, shook his head, and then looked away, clearing his throat as he did so.

"I should return you to your mother," he muttered, his free hand settling on hers for just a moment as she held it on his arm. "No doubt news of our courtship will be all around London by the morning."

"I expect it shall be." There was a tremor in her voice as she thought of the many interesting remarks that would be made. "We can do nothing other than accept it, I suppose."

Lord Kentmore stopped short. He did not turn to her but instead, looked directly ahead, only to sigh and then glance towards her.

"I..." Trailing off, he closed his eyes. "I am sorry, Charlotte."

Whether it was the fact that he said her name, or that he had apologized with evident sincerity, Charlotte did not know. But something within her lifted, then, something that made her heart catapult against her ribs. She swallowed, trying to find something to say, but no words came. Lord Kentmore offered her a small nod, as though he was now glad that he had said what he desired, only to then lead her forward again, returning her to her mother.

It was the most astonishing thing, Charlotte considered, as she came to stand beside her mother once more. Both she and Lord Kentmore had been upset and frustrated and yet, in a single moment, she had found that releasing from her a little – though not entirely – simply because of his apology.

"Did you enjoy your time with Lord Kentmore?" Lady Morton beamed at Charlotte though she herself struggled to smile. "It will be the talk of London very soon, I am sure!"

"It seems that it shall be," Charlotte answered, feeling herself a little weary now, not quite certain that she could cope with all that the *ton* would put to her. "And somehow, I shall have to face it all."

CHAPTER TEN

Andrew paced up and down his study, his mind tormented. No matter what he did, he could not get his thoughts free from Miss Hawick. The sadness that had been within her when they had spoken at the soiree – a soiree which had been some two evenings ago – had hit him hard, and the weight of his guilt had seemed to increase significantly to the point that he had struggled to bear up beneath it. Yes, he still had the frustration of being unable to continue to live just as he pleased, the upset of being forced to wed when he did not want to do such a thing, but the realization of just what he had done to Miss Hawick had broken apart all of that. Now, he found himself deeply sorrowful, filled with regret, and troubled with the guilt and shame that seemed to want to remind him of his foolishness at every moment.

He had not stepped out into society since that soiree. Lord Glenfield had come to call, but Andrew had told him that he was not feeling particularly well, and needed to rest and, thus, his friend had taken his leave. It had been an excuse, of course, for Andrew was quite well, within himself. For some reason, he simply did not want to have any sort of company.

"What can be done?"

Walking up to the window of his study and looking out at the street below, Andrew took in the carriages and the passers-by, knowing full well that most of them would be speaking of his connection to Miss Hawick. Lord Glenfield had been the one to inform him that the *ton* was now full of whisperings and the like about his courtship of the lady – with some questioning whether or not he really meant it – and that had brought Andrew no pleasure whatsoever. Instead, he had shrunk back from it, deciding to hide himself away for a short while, simply so that he could avoid the *ton*'s scrutiny – though it could not be avoided forever.

Closing his eyes, Andrew dropped his head to the glass of the window, feeling the cool sensation of it against his skin. In only a few days, his entire life had been altered. That had been the consequences of his own actions but, at the same time, it had pulled Miss Hawick in with him. She'd had no say in the matter, had been forced into this marriage because of what he had done – and she was broken-hearted over it.

Andrew lifted his head from the glass, disliking the fact that his heart was so pained over the lady. He did not want to be affected by her, did not want to find himself troubled because of her sadness and yet, he could not help it. What was worse was that, yes, she did not want to marry him, but he recognized that it was because of his character, because of who he was, that she was so sorrowful. He was not a kind fellow, he was not a considerate or generous sort. What she had leveled at him during their brief conversation at the soiree had been quite true, he *was* selfish and arrogant, thinking of no one but himself. Having any thoughts of others, or permitting himself to be concerned about them, was not something which he had ever dwelt upon.

But now, he was being forced to.

Sighing, Andrew turned around and made his way back to the middle of the drawing-room, flinging himself down onto one of the couches, only to rise again and shove one hand through his hair. Why could he not forget about her? Why was it that her sadness had such an effect on him? It was not as though he could do anything about it now, it was not as if he would be able to change their circumstances. She was to be courted by him, he would soon propose, and they would, once the banns had been called, wed.

But I could attempt to be a little kinder. More considerate. She is to be my wife, after all! Are we always to be this fraught? Or could I, in accepting this, in accepting her, try to be more thoughtful of her emotions? Yes, she sees me as I truly am... might there be a way where I could change that. Would that not make for a better relationship between us? After all, if I am to take her as my wife, I must be considering our future.

He swallowed as a tightness came into his throat, thinking of his future. What would it be like to have her by his side, always sorrowful, always broken-hearted, always despondent? *I do not think I could bear it,* he thought to himself, raking his other hand through his hair, fully aware it now was a wild mop rather than carefully placed. *I may not like this circumstance, but I do not want Charlotte to be sorrowful every day of our marriage.*

Andrew dropped his hand back to his side, acknowledging to himself that he could certainly attempt to be a little more amiable in his interactions with her, instead of letting his frustration and upset rule his tongue. With a scowl, he found his legs taking him to his writing desk and, sitting down, put his hand to the quill.

He did not know what it was that he wanted to write. All he could see was Miss Hawick's blue eyes filled with tears as she looked back at him, the single teardrop falling to her cheek. The pain in her eyes, the sadness in her expression, and the brokenness of her heart cried out to him. Dipping the quill into the ink, the words began to flow.

Weariness haunts your inner soul,
The pain of a heart shattered.
My cold fingers placed it there,
Stealing away your joy.
Purposeless or purposeful,
Our path remains the same.
We are bound and we are tied,
Never again to be free.
There is no respite from the pain,
Your heart is heavy still.
I own it all, my regret severe,
The darkness like my shadow.

. . .

He lifted the quill and blinked, staring down at the words on the page. He had never written anything like that before, had never once merely opened his heart and let it speak. Those words were the very story going on with his heart, the description of all he was feeling. Closing his eyes, Andrew took a breath and then, after a moment, continued to write.

~

"Miss Hawick, Lady Morton, Miss Hawick."

Andrew inclined his head as the lady to whom he was paying his attentions descended from the carriage, though she did not look up into his face. Rather, she kept her gaze to the left, bobbing a curtsey as she did so.

"Good afternoon, Lord Kentmore." Perhaps catching the way that Lady Morton lifted one eyebrow very carefully, Miss Hawick continued quickly, though there was no hint of happiness in either her expression or her voice. "It was very kind of you to invite me out for a walk through St James' Park."

"We are courting now, Miss Hawick, are we not?" Andrew offered her his arm, giving a smile to Lady Morton who returned it with a nod, as though to say that she trusted him with her daughter, as Miss Lillian Hawick simply smiled. "I must spend as much time with you as I can."

Lady Morton beamed at him with this remark though Miss Hawick did not respond, aside from taking his arm. Together, they strolled into the park a little more, with

Lady Morton and her other daughter following after them a short distance away.

"You say such pretty things in front of my mother while, at the very same time, giving no clear explanation to me as to why you have been absent from society for almost a sennight!" Miss Hawick's voice was low, but there was a hint of upset in it. "I have had many a person coming to speak to me about my courtship and they have asked me where you are, given that you have not been present, and I have had no answer to give them!"

Shame flung itself in Andrew's face.

"Forgive me. I needed some time to consider a good many things."

"I see." She shook her head. "And evidently, it was too much for you to consider even writing me a short note to inform me of it? You can imagine that there have been some... whispers... as to where you might be, and why you might have removed yourself from society."

Andrew closed his eyes briefly, realizing now that he had never once thought of what might happen during his time away from society.

"I did not imagine for a moment that anything would be said."

"You mean to say that you did not think about the situation at all. You know as well as I that society likes to whisper about anything it can and, it was more than willing to speak of my courtship with a rogue – a rogue who, some said, went to Bath simply to escape me, realizing that he had made a mistake!"

Guilt wrapped around his heart and Andrew swallowed thickly.

"I am sorry for my lack of consideration. I needed some time to think about our circumstances, to really consider what it is that has happened between us and what must now occur. It has taken me some time to, first of all, accept it and, thereafter, to consider how I must behave."

She looked at him.

"And what have you decided?"

Andrew drew himself up.

"Miss Hawick, I think it important to inform you that I have come to a decision as regards our future."

Miss Hawick's expression did not change, her fair curls blowing gently in the wind.

"I see. And what decision is that? Is it that you shall end the courtship regardless, and leave me without any reputation whatsoever?"

Her harsh reaction had him scowling, and he was about to fire some hard words back towards her, only to remind himself of just how troubled she must be at present. That was the reason for her response, the reason for her upset and he was not about to make it worse.

"I promise you, Miss Hawick, I will never do any such thing as that." His hand found itself upon hers, just as it had done at the soiree, though he kept his fingers there for only a few moments, not wishing for her to react badly to his touch. "I am committed to this connection, you understand. I do not like how it has come about – as I am certain you do not either – but in considering it all, I have concluded that there is very little point in fighting it. Therefore, Miss Hawick, I should like to do all that I can to know you better, not just because I might one day be forced to answer questions from the *ton,* but also because I would like to know the lady who is to be my wife." Seeing the way her eyes widened, Andrew offered her a small smile, praying that she would not reject him immediately, not when it had taken him such a long time to come to this point. It had been near a sennight now since the soiree and, given that he had remained in his townhouse for those days, thinking and considering, he wanted very much for Miss Hawick to see that he was genuine in his request.

Miss Hawick frowned.

"You think that you will be able to charm me, Lord Kentmore?"

"Charm you?"

She nodded, her tone icy.

"You are just as much a rogue as you ever were. I am sure that you will try anything to make me feel a little warmer towards you, will you not?" A hint of color came into her cheeks as she spoke, her chin lifting. "I am not about to be taken in."

Again, anger struck hard at Andrew's heart, but he fought it back, reminding himself of the pain and the sorrow which must be very present in her heart. It was a most unusual sensation, for he had never once done such a thing before and indeed, it was a battle but, as he looked into her face and saw the gentle glint of tears in her eyes, his heart ached with regret all over again.

"I can understand why you might think that I am not at all to be trusted," he said, slowly. "But I have been considering these last few days and considering severely." He swallowed tightly, then looked at her. "I do not want you to be sorrowful with every day that passes, Miss Hawick. If there is a way for us to move forward to a situation where we can, at least, tolerate each other, I should be glad to find it."

Miss Hawick glanced at him, though Andrew caught the slight tremble about her lips.

"I do not know if such a thing can be. I fear that you will always be angry that I have taken away your freedom and I, mayhap, shall always be upset that such a thing occurred... and that I did not respond as I ought to have done."

Andrew looked at her sharply.

"Whatever do you mean? You behaved perfectly well and–"

"I did not." Miss Hawick's eyes glinted as though she were holding back tears, though her voice remained steady. "I recognize that there is blame here, Lord Kentmore, not just with you but also with myself."

Andrew shook his head, a little surprised at her words, but feeling them stab a sharp stake into his conscience.

"No, indeed, Miss Hawick. There is no guilt on your part. None whatsoever."

"Yes, there is." She turned, stopping sharply and pulling her hand from his arm. "Had I pulled back, had I exclaimed aloud, then my sister would never have seen anything, would never have insisted that we wed. Do you not understand, Lord Kentmore? Just because you have the burden of responsibility does not mean that a similar responsibility has not set itself upon my shoulders also! I should have made it perfectly clear to you that I was *not* who you thought me to be and, mayhap then, I might have been spared all of this. *We* might have been spared this."

Shaking his head, his throat closing up at the pain in her eyes, Andrew grasped both of her hands in his and leaned closer to her, a vehemence in his chest that threatened to explode at any moment.

"I shall not have you bear any responsibility for this in any way, Miss Hawick, not for one moment. You must understand, this is entirely *my* doing and whether you ought to have moved away or not has no bearing. I cannot imagine what must have happened at that moment. You cannot blame yourself for the shock and the fright which captured you, I will not have it." He pressed her hands. "Please. I can see that this has already caused you a great deal of pain and to have this burden upon yourself when you have no reason to carry it must only be adding to that."

Miss Hawick sniffed lightly but kept her gaze steady, looking back at him though she remained silent. Andrew said nothing further, waiting for her to respond, waiting for her to wrestle through what it was he had said. Then, slowly, she pulled her hands out of his.

"I appreciate that you are willing to take on the sole responsibility," she said, making to walk along the path again rather than standing opposite him. "Your concern for my welfare is surprising but appreciated."

Andrew's lips quirked, reminding himself that Miss Hawick was blunt in her honesty though, mayhap, he would have to become used to that.

"I did hear you when you told me that I was

nothing but arrogant and selfish," he said, as she blushed furiously, looking away. "You are not mistaken, Miss Hawick. I will, however, attempt to be more considerate of you, since we are to be husband and wife."

Her blue eyes caught his.

"Though you still intend to return to your... appetites once we are returned from our wedding trip."

The statement made him recoil. He did not know what to say, for part of him wanted to be very clear indeed that he would do whatever he wished, whenever he wished to do it while, yet at the very same time, the thought of the agony of such a thing would bring to her silenced him from saying those words. Instead, he took a deep breath, shrugged, and chose to say nothing, though he caught the way that she slumped a little at his response before drawing herself up again.

"Oh, good afternoon! How unexpected to see you out, Lord Kentmore! I did not know that you had recovered."

Andrew smiled briefly.

"Lord Glenfield, good afternoon. This is the first day that I have ventured out of my townhouse."

"Recovered?" Miss Hawick glanced at Andrew and then back to Lord Glenfield. "I do not understand."

Lord Glenfield gestured to Andrew, his smile warm.

"Lord Kentmore informed me that he was unwell. I am glad to see that it was not long-lasting."

Miss Hawick's lips pursed.

"I see."

"Might I ask if you are here for a purpose?" Andrew

asked quickly, attempting to change the course of the conversation. "Or have you just come to take the air?"

A broad smile crossed Lord Glenfield's face.

"I have come to see if I might walk with Miss Lillian Hawick for a time. She informed me that she would be here this afternoon, and I saw my opportunity to further my connection." He tipped his head, looking at Andrew carefully. "I have also a copy of The London Chronicle in which there is another poem. Miss Hawick informed me previously that she was most interested in them, so I must hope that she finds this one to be just as intriguing, though it is markedly different from the others."

"Different?"

Andrew's surprise sent pins and needles through his frame, hearing Miss Hawick's interest. He said nothing, however, casting Lord Glenfield a sharp look that told him, he prayed, to say nothing about Andrew being the author.

A small nod came from Lord Glenfield, though he turned his attention directly to Miss Hawick.

"Yes, indeed, it is very changed from the previous poems." He held out the paper to her. "Should you like to read it?"

Something flared in Andrew's chest at the way that Miss Hawick hesitated, finding himself eagerly desiring her to take hold of the paper and read the words he had written. Despite telling himself repeatedly that he did not care what she thought of them, his heart hoped that she would find something in it to approve of.

Eventually, she took it.

Andrew's heart began to pound as she found the

poem and, bending her head, began to read. He shifted a little so as to make out her expression, seeing the way that her blue eyes rounded at the edges, how her eyebrows lifted and, in observing that, he let a broad smile spread across his face.

Lord Glenfield cleared his throat, and Andrew quickly snapped that smile from his face, realizing just how close he had come to giving himself away.

"Well." Miss Hawick handed the paper back to Lord Glenfield, her lips curving into a soft smile. "I think that my sister may be a little disappointed, for it does not speak fervently of love, as the other ones have done."

She glanced at Andrew, then let her gaze fall to the ground, her hands clasping lightly in front of her. Andrew, a little confused, frowned, only for the realization of what she was thinking to become shockingly clear to him. She was remaining silent, keeping her thoughts and her opinions to herself, evidently believing that he had no interest in hearing what she had to say. Yet again, another swell of regret crashed into him, and he gestured to her, trying to smile.

"Please, do tell us your thoughts, Miss Hawick."

Her eyes caught his for a brief moment.

"Are you quite certain that you wish to hear my opinion?"

Lord Glenfield chuckled.

"Even if he does not, I should be glad to."

This made Miss Hawick smile and, much to Andrew's surprise, jealousy ran right through him, stealing his breath for a moment. He blinked and then looked away, frowning hard at his own, unexpected, reaction.

"Then I shall say that I think it a most unexpected poem, so different from the others that I wonder if it is by the same author!" Miss Hawick spread out her hands. "This does not speak of love, not in the way that one would expect, at least, but there is certainly a good deal of honesty within those words, I think." Her hands fell back to her sides. "To my mind, it has a greater reach in its emotion, speaking truth through carefully chosen words. I think I prefer it to the other poems thus far - though, as I have said, I do not know if it is by the same author."

"It is."

The words flung themselves from Andrew's mouth before he could prevent them, seeing not only Miss Hawick looking at him in surprise but also Lord Glenfield, clearly astonished that he was being so bold.

"That is to say, I know who the author is, and I can assure you, it is the very same person," Andrew clarified, heat beginning to build in his chest and spread up towards his neck. "I am certain that he will be glad to hear that you have enjoyed it, Miss Hawick. How the *ton* shall consider it remains to be seen!"

"And with that, I must take my leave and speak with your sister, Miss Hawick." Lord Glenfield smiled and inclined his head. "Good afternoon."

Andrew stepped back towards Miss Hawick and, almost before he had offered her his arm, her hand had reached towards him, as though she was now expecting him to be there. A small smile played about his lips as they began to walk together again, and he felt as though a bridge had begun to be built between them, as though a vast chasm was slowly being closed. Thinking of her reaction to his poem made that smile grow all the more and, though the silence between them continued, Andrew's heart lifted with a sense of contentment and happiness.

It was all most extraordinary.

CHAPTER ELEVEN

Ten days later.

"You and I have been spending a good deal of our time together these last few days."

Charlotte turned to glance into Lord Kentmore's eyes, finding her senses stirred whenever she did so.

"Yes, that is true."

"Tell me." He winked at her, and instantly, Charlotte's entire body felt itself engulfed in flame. "Am I at all improved in your opinion?"

The heat which had been in Charlotte's frame now rose into her cheeks. She was not quite certain what to say and instead, turned her attention back to the rows of books before them.

"It is a strange thing to want to know, Lord Kentmore."

The gentleman chuckled, making Charlotte smile

despite her own sense of uncertainty. Her reactions to Lord Kentmore were becoming more and more altered with every minute spent in his company though she did not want to make him aware of that. Nor, in fact, did she even want to admit it to herself!

"It may show my arrogance, yes?" Lord Kentmore sighed heavily. "I suppose that is not something I had considered." The smile on his lips began to fade away, though his gaze lingered on hers. "Truth be told, Miss Hawick, I find myself in a state which I never once dreamed I would be in. I am no longer acting as a rogue but instead I am committed only to one courtship! I understand that our connection was not something you desired, was not something that you hoped for, but all the same, given that we are now bound together, I wondered if you had felt any happier. That is what my concern is."

Much to Charlotte's surprise, his hand reached out and caught hers, though it was only for a moment. She blinked quickly, turning her head away from his, finding their connected gaze a little too intense, given all that she was now feeling. Could she believe him in this? Could she be certain that what he said truly was genuine? Did he really consider her happiness, or was it that he was seeking only to improve himself in her opinion in the hope of garnering her contentment for when he chose to return to his roguish ways?

"You are going to remain silent and leave my heart to suffer, I see." Lord Kentmore sighed heavily and put one hand to his heart. "It is just as the poem said in The London Chronicle, *'the ache of my heart is constant and prolonged, the path before me lit by my wrongs.'*"

Charlotte laughed softly, finding the strength to look back at him without her face burning hot.

"Very well, Lord Kentmore," she said, turning to face him. "Yes, I am a little happier. You appear not to be as despicable a character as I first thought you."

Lord Kentmore winced but grinned.

"That is comforting, I think."

"I did not expect you to have a love of art," Charlotte continued, as his eyes searched hers. "That has been interesting to me."

"Aside from my shooting and gambling, yes?"

Lord Kentmore smiled and tilted his head, his eyes twinkling.

"Yes, aside from that," Charlotte laughed, only for her breath to hitch as Lord Kentmore moved a little closer, his gaze seeming to soften, the curve of his lips a little more gentle.

This was what they had spent their time doing these last few days, walking together, taking tea together, but mostly, talking together. It had not been easy, for the first few visits had been strained and difficult, but the more time Charlotte had been in his company, the easier it had become, to the point that now, Charlotte's desire to move closer to him was becoming harder and harder to resist.

"I may not be as terrible a gentleman as you first feared, then?" Lord Kentmore's voice was quieter now, his gaze gentling as he leaned his head down just a little. "You are not as upset as you once were at the thought of marrying me?"

Charlotte swallowed tightly, lifting her gaze to his,

though for some reason, her eyes went to settle against his lips.

"I do not think that you are entirely dreadful, no," she whispered, the awareness that they were very much alone – despite the fact that her mother was in the bookshop also – making her tremble with a sudden anticipation.

Lord Kentmore smiled but, after another moment, lifted his head and stepped away.

"That is good." His tone had become a little more formal now, a tad more clipped as he turned his head away. "I am glad to hear you say such a thing, Miss Hawick."

Within a few moments, the heat in Charlotte's frame had run from her and was replaced, instead, with a chill that washed over her. She blinked, a little confused at what had just taken place, and with some regret, attempted to look at the books rather than dwell on the present state of her heart.

∼

"You say that he has become a little more considerate?"

Charlotte nodded, her lips twisting for a moment before she spoke.

"He has, I will admit. Not only that, but we have spent a good many hours in company with each other and I have begun to find him... interesting."

Miss Marshall blinked.

"Interesting?"

"There is more to his character than I first thought,"

Charlotte answered, trying to explain. "We have spoken of his interests and yes, though he thinks mostly of riding and shooting, he has expressed some thoughts about reading that I enjoy and has also many a thought on art."

Her friend's surprise showed in her wide eyes, making Charlotte smile ruefully.

"Truly?"

"Truly. Though I must confess, it is difficult to recall at times how roguish he is," Charlotte continued, sighing heavily. "It is easy to see just how readily so many of the ladies of London gave themselves up to his charms."

Miss Marshall looped her arm through Charlotte's.

"You may reform him yet."

A laugh broke through between them and Charlotte shook her head.

"I do not know if such a thing is possible!"

Her friend looked at her.

"But should you like it to be?"

Without hesitation, Charlotte nodded.

"The thought of marrying a rogue is bad enough, but to know that he might continue to pursue the affections of others thereafter is painful indeed." Her voice softened. "I have not spoken with him about that as yet, but I think I shall."

Miss Marshall's eyes flickered with curiosity.

"Might I ask if your hope of that comes solely from a desire to have a devoted husband? Or if there is something more there?"

"What do you mean?"

Miss Marshall smiled, a hint of pink in her cheeks.

"Only to suggest that you might have that desire also

because you have begun to have an affection for him, to truly care for him."

Charlotte opened her mouth to refute it, only to close it again. She thought for some moments and then shook her head, sighing heavily.

"I do not know. I do not *want* to have any feelings for him, for then I might find myself overwhelmed with affection while he pushes me aside, and that would only make my situation worse."

"Then you must ask him," Miss Marshall suggested, quickly. "Ask him as to whether or not you can have what you desire: a husband who is singularly devoted to his wife, regardless of what he feels." She smiled again and lifted her shoulders in a small shrug. "That way, you will be able to know whether or not you can let your heart free to grow in its affection for him, or whether you should seek to bring it to an immediate end."

Charlotte nodded slowly, seeing the wisdom in her friend's words.

"I thank you, Sarah," she said, softly. "You are quite right. I must speak to him just as soon as I am able. That way, I shall know for sure."

CHAPTER TWELVE

Andrew made his way into Lord Childers' house, nodding and smiling at various other guests, all of whom he was acquainted with. There came one or two knowing looks, one or two gentle, teasing smiles, but Andrew did not respond to any of them. Instead, he greeted his host, took a glass of whisky from the tray held by the footman, and then made his way directly towards Lord Glenfield.

"Good evening." He gestured to the rest of the room. "It is quite a crush, is it not?"

Lord Glenfield chuckled.

"It is just as I expected it would be. Lord Childers is known for inviting far too many guests and then cramming them all into his townhouse, though I believe he has opened the library, the parlor, the terrace, and even the gardens, so there should be a quieter room somewhere. Though you are not particularly inclined towards quieter spaces, are you?"

Andrew winced, though he grinned back at Lord Glenfield at the same time.

"I may not have always been, no," he said, with a chuckle. "Though I should go in search of Miss Hawick, I think."

"Oh, they are unable to attend this evening." Lord Glenfield lifted his shoulders in a shrug as Andrew shot him a frown. "Miss Lillian Hawick informed me that they were attending Lord and Lady Rutton's card party this evening."

"Oh." Disappointment settled in Andrew's chest, and he frowned at the sensation, disliking it intensely. "I did not know."

Lord Glenfield's lip curved, a knowing look in his eye.

"You are sorrowful that she will not be in attendance."

"Sorrowful?" Andrew scoffed, shaking his head. "Not in the least."

His friend grinned but said nothing more and yet, that knowing look on his face remained. Andrew tried to ignore it and, much to his relief, was soon lost in conversation with two other gentlemen who came to speak with him though, much to his frustration, Miss Hawick still lingered in the back of his mind.

I almost kissed her again in the bookshop.

It had been a most extraordinary – and most astonishing – thing for him to want to do and, though he had managed to resist it, though he had managed to pull back before he had done such a thing, that urge had lingered long within him.

"How goes your courtship, Lord Kentmore?"

Andrew pulled himself out of his thoughts, looking to Lord Telford.

"My courtship is going very well, I thank you."

Lord Telford's eyebrows lifted.

"Indeed? Then you are not about to bring that to an end?"

A gentle frown pulled at Andrew's forehead.

"End my courtship of Miss Hawick?"

The gentleman nodded just as Andrew shook his head, a little surprised at how the thought distressed him.

"I have no intention of doing so, no."

"Then you might consider betrothal?" the other fellow said, as Andrew's frown grew darker, his heart squeezing.

"I think that is something that the Marquess can decide for himself, including when it is that he wishes to speak of it."

Much to Andrew's relief, Lord Glenfield came to Andrew's rescue, so that he did not have to give any sort of explanation.

"Though you must see how extraordinary it is for you to now be courting a young lady!" Lord Telford interjected, just as Andrew had been about to change the conversation entirely. "You were behaving just as you always have done, up until a few weeks ago, and now you are entirely altered! Little wonder that there are some who are saying that your absence from society once that announcement had been made was an indication that you had no real interest in the lady. That is why they are now waiting for you to make an end of the courtship, given that, by now, you have probably enjoyed all the fun that you can take from that connection."

Andrew scowled.

"I do not behave improperly in any way with Miss Hawick," he said, a twist of anger in his voice which made the smile on Lord Telford's face crumple. "Be assured of that."

Lord Telford looked away and a strained silence grew between them, making Andrew's face grow hot. With a look at Lord Glenfield, he excused himself from the group, quite certain that there would be more conversation about him after he had left.

The situation with Miss Hawick was something that he was trying very hard to put from his mind, though he was struggling to do so, unfortunately. The way that she had looked into his eyes, the desire within him to pull her close, and the connection between them which had been developing in its intensity, was making his heart yearn for even more of the same. Yes, he had always wanted to pull various young ladies into his arms, and had done so multiple times and on various occasions, but with Miss Hawick, it appeared to be quite different.

"Though when she asked me if I would give up my roguish interests, I did not consent," he reminded himself aloud, making his way to the gardens in the hope that the cool night air might calm his mind and his hot cheeks. "I do not *have* to do anything. I did not want to wed in the first place! If I wish to, then I can go back to being as I have always been once our wedding trip is at an end. There is nothing wrong with that!"

Those words did nothing other than spike guilt in his

heart. With a low groan – and ignoring the looks of those around him – Andrew strode out of the French doors and into the dark of the gardens, glass still in hand.

I do not want this.

His heart fought back at him as he told himself, repeatedly, that he felt nothing for Miss Hawick and that his desire to return to being a rogue was not only true but understandable. After all, he had never wanted to wed and was being forced to do so and Miss Hawick knew precisely the sort of gentleman he was.

Andrew hung his head, coming to stand just beside a small fountain, the moonlight dancing on the water.

But I am changing. I am not the same as I was when I first kissed her.

Letting out a long sigh, Andrew lifted his glass to his lips and drained the amber liquid, hoping that it would bring him some relief. He had enjoyed speaking with Miss Hawick about his interest in art – an interest which he had not pursued in some time – as well as listening to her speak with such passion about the written word. There was more than just a physical connection between them and that frightened him, for it was beginning to alter him in a way that he had not expected. The thought of bringing her pain, of seeing it shine in her eyes, was even more unbearable than it had been when he had written that poem. Could he really turn back to the rogue he had been?

"I do not want to change."

Rebelling against his own heart, Andrew took another breath and made to turn around, intending to go back into the house and find something to do, whether it be cards or simply conversation so that he could forget entirely about Miss Hawick.

Someone came to stand in his way.

"Lord Kentmore. I am sorry to hear that you are now courting a young lady."

Andrew blinked, recognizing the voice of the lady before him, though he struggled to make out her features. Their host had opened up the garden, yes, but he had not thought to light it in any way.

"There is no need to feel any sort of sympathy for me, I assure you."

The lady laughed softly, her hand going to his chest in such a familiar way, that Andrew knew that he had shared a connection with her previously.

Inwardly, he pulled away from her, taking a small step back so that her hand fell away.

"You are being very good about it all." Lady Faustine's voice was gentle, almost tender. "No doubt there is a reason that you are courting her, for I know that you, being as you are, would never have willingly turned to marriage. I do hope that it was not my tardiness at the ball that brought this circumstance to you?"

Realizing that it was Lady Faustine he spoke with, Andrew let out a slow breath.

"Lady Faustine, good evening. Yes, I am sorry that we did not meet that evening."

Andrew frowned as he spoke, realizing that he was not sorry in the least, though the words were spoken regardless.

"That was the evening that your courtship with this Miss Hawick became apparent." Lady Faustine tilted her head. "There must be a reason for it. We have not had a chance to speak about that, as yet, but I presume that it is because you were found in a somewhat compromising position? One that you cannot now escape from?" She laughed softly as Andrew frowned heavily. "You are not the first scoundrel to have been caught so."

"Indeed."

With a shake of his head, Andrew made to sidestep her, but Lady Faustine put out one hand, catching him.

"Come now, Lord Kentmore! You cannot tell me that you will willingly turn away from me now, merely because you are courting?" Her hand went to his shoulder, then lifted to his neck as she came closer to him. "We have not yet shared any sort of connection this Season. I have been seeking a time to find you, to be alone with you, and this is the moment that has presented itself – and I have been waiting for a very long time." Andrew swallowed tightly, confused at his own reluctance. Had he not been eagerly looking forward to stealing Lady Faustine into his arms only a short while ago? Why now was he feeling as though he ought to push her away and, thereafter, step back into the house, leaving her in the darkness? "Lord Kentmore, you are a little reluctant, I think!" Lady Faustine's laughter made Andrew wince, his heart shadowed as he fought to find clarity. "It cannot be because you are afraid to be seen, given that the gardens are lit only by moonlight. Come now, do not push yourself away from me simply because you are courting another! I know – all without you saying a word – that there is no genuine interest there. The Marquess I know would never permit himself to be so lost to matrimony!"

Andrew steeled himself, pushing away his conflicting thoughts as best he could.

"You are quite right, Maria," he said, using her forename given the connection they had once shared. "I have never wanted this situation for myself."

"Then there can be no reason for you *not* to permit yourself the same freedom as before," she murmured, her breath hot against his cheek. "No reason whatsoever."

Before Andrew could say a word, before he could protest, the lady had lifted her head, stood on her tiptoes, and pressed her lips to his – and Andrew recoiled in one, intense moment. It was as though his body reacted without his awareness, pushing her back from him and stumbling back into the darkness of the garden, his stomach twisting and his body going hot and then cold immediately thereafter. A sense of revulsion overpowered him, and he wiped his mouth furiously with the back of his hand over and over again.

"What are you doing?" Lady Faustine's voice was high-pitched as Andrew resisted the urge to spit hard on the ground, as though that might help him remove every single trace of her from him. "Why did you push me away?"

"I do not want this." Andrew's words tore harshly from his lips, disgust still rearing its head within him – disgust at both his previous actions that had brought her to him in that way, as well as her present determinations. Shame at his weakness thrust itself through his heart and he closed his eyes, his chest heaving. "Never again, Lady Faustine. *Never.*"

There came silence for a long moment, only for the lady to come towards him, one finger pressing hard into his chest.

"This is because of *her*," she hissed, her anger clear. "It is because of what she has done to you that you now turn away from me! What is it that she has said? Is there some hold on you that I cannot know of? Some promise, some whisper that binds you to her in a way that you cannot free yourself from?"

Andrew shook his head, taking another step back. He could not explain it himself, could not find a way to understand it but yet, all the same, the thought of taking Lady Faustine into his arms again made him almost nauseous.

"I cannot ever be to you as I have been," he said, a little hoarsely. "Never again."

Lady Faustine lifted her chin, her eyes glittering in the moonlight.

"You are rejecting me."

"I am telling you that I will not be as I have been to you," Andrew stated, a sense of relief flooding him as though he knew that this was exactly what it was that he needed to do. "What we shared, it is now at an end, Lady Faustine."

"But... but what if I do not wish it to be?" Lady Faustine's voice held a tone of slight desperation now, though Andrew could only shake his head. "What then?"

He spread out both hands.

"That means nothing to me, Lady Faustine, not any

longer. I cannot continue in this way, not any longer." Dropping his hands back to his sides, he stepped away from her. "Good evening."

"Wait!"

Her hand was on his arm, but Andrew pushed it back, moving away from her as quickly as he could and feeling his satisfaction growing with every step.

CHAPTER THIRTEEN

"Should you like me to read it to you?"

A little surprised at Lord Kentmore's offer, Charlotte took a moment before she answered.

"You would like to read the poem to me?"

Lord Kentmore shrugged.

"I do not see why not. I am able to read, Miss Hawick, in case you were uncertain about that."

Charlotte laughed, only to pull the sound back into herself. These last few days with Lord Kentmore had brought a significant change in his manner towards her, and the ease of their conversations had brought about something of a softness within her. Try as she might, she could not hold onto the anger and the frustration which she had once held so near.

"Well?"

Lord Kentmore tipped his head, one eyebrow lifting, and Charlotte's breath hitched, uneven in her chest as the gold in his eyes seemed to swirl, bringing a fresh awareness to her of just how handsome he was.

Be careful, Charlotte, she reminded herself, sitting up straight and reaching for her tea. *He is still a rogue yet.*

"If you wish to read it, Lord Kentmore, I will listen to you," she said, trying to keep the smile from her face. "I do hope that you read well."

He grinned at her and her heart leaped, betraying her.

"I believe that you must be the judge of that, Miss Hawick, and you give your opinion very decisively, do you not? I will not be in any doubt as to whether I read well or not once I hear it!"

At this, Charlotte could not help but smile.

"At least you know me well enough to understand that," she said, seeing a twinkle come into his eyes. "Very well, Lord Kentmore. I shall listen and I shall give you my thoughts thereafter – on both the poem and the reading."

Lord Kentmore chuckled, picked up the paper, and rose to his feet. They were quite alone in the drawing room, albeit with the maid in the corner, the door open, and her Mama's promise to return to them within a few minutes, but it gave Lord Kentmore ample time to read this new poem to her. There had been three new poems in The London Chronicle since the last one that Charlotte had thought well of, each changed from the first she had read. It was as though the author was beginning to step forward, to consider his true emotions, to speak of them with great honesty, and she found that to be rather refreshing.

"Then I shall begin." Lord Kentmore cleared his throat, his eyes on the paper and a seriousness beginning to fill his expression, pulling his smile away. "A poem from the anonymous gentleman." Taking a breath, Lord Kentmore set back his shoulders and then began.

"I am a ship, sailing the vast, open sea,
The horse which runs wild, freedom in its veins.
Yet, I feel myself constrained,
The wind pulling me, filling my sails,
A scent of home and happiness begging me to return.
To throw aside such freedom, can I bear to do it?
To set my feet to an as yet untrodden path,
But one which will determine it forevermore?
There is but one thing which can demand it of me.
One thing that cries out to make itself known.
The whisper on the wind is your voice.
The scent in the air, your sweet perfume.
Can I give it all to you?

Or will I take to my heels and search freedom once more?"

Charlotte did not speak for some moments. Instead, she let the words sink into her soul, her eyes having already closed as Lord Kentmore read. There was something about the poem which spoke to her, something which reached out and called to her heart. Lord Kentmore's voice had held a gentleness to it which she had never heard before, a sweetness to it which had reverberated in her very soul. She had never expected him to be able to read with such delicacy, with such tenderness, and yet, it was as though he had written each and every word and was filling it with his own emotions.

"I do hope that my reading was satisfactory for you."

Opening her eyes, Charlotte let out a small sigh, then smiled at him.

"I must say, I am astonished."

Lord Kentmore looked at her, then much to Charlotte's surprise, came to sit beside her, a fervency in his gaze which she had not expected to be there.

"Astonished?"

"Yes," she answered, a strange swirling in her core at his nearness. "I did not think that you would read so well, Lord Kentmore."

He closed his eyes for a moment, ducked his head, and then smiled.

"I am very glad to hear it."

And I did not think that he would be so affected by my consideration of him.

"The poem was beautiful," she continued, as he looked back at her. "It held such feeling, I confess that my heart was stirred."

"Truly?" Lord Kentmore's hand settled on hers, though he did not ever lift his gaze away from her face, and Charlotte started in surprise, her heart quickening. "You thought well of it?"

Blinking quickly, Charlotte looked away, licking her lips as all manner of emotions began to climb through her.

"I did, truly." She managed to turn her gaze back to him. "You know the author, yes? I am sure that he must be pleased that there are so many young ladies in London who are eager for his poetry."

"Mayhap, though not all of them are as discerning as you, I am sure," came the reply, his hand never lifting from hers, his hazel eyes searching her face. "My dear

Miss Hawick, to know that I have pleased you means a great deal."

Charlotte said nothing, finding herself drawn to him in a way that was most disconcerting, appreciating that he valued her opinion of his reading of the poem. She had no desire to pull her hand away, no thought of rising from her chair to put the appropriate distance between them. Instead, the thought came to her of the first time he had kissed her and, without meaning to, her eyes went to his lips. What would it feel like to have them pressed to hers again? Would there be the same passion as there had been when he had thought her to be someone else?

"Miss Hawick," Lord Kentmore breathed, leaning a little closer to her. "I must ask you if–"

He is still a rogue.

"Might I ask if you still have every intention of returning to your previous interests once we are wed?" Ice washed over her as Lord Kentmore pulled back, his hand taken from hers at the very same moment. The thought of their kiss had brought to mind the fact that he had been intending to kiss someone *else* and, with that, the realization that she was being nothing but foolish in thinking of him in any way other than as a rogue. "You and I have become a little closer these last few days, Lord Kentmore, but that does not change the fact that you are determined to be a rogue still, once we are wed – or whenever you decide to return to it."

Lord Kentmore frowned, a shadow coming over his expression.

"What is it that you want me to say, Miss Hawick? I have already assured you that I will not do so."

"For the time being," she stated, angry with herself for letting her feelings become affected by him. "You know very well that I do not wish to marry a rogue."

"Yes, you have made that very clear."

Charlotte took a breath, a sudden sense of desperation beginning to flood her.

"What I want is to hear you state that you will be as any gentleman ought to be when he is wed: singularly devoted to his wife."

Lord Kentmore looked back at her for a long moment. Nothing was said between them, no words came from his mouth and Charlotte had none to say either. Eventually, Lord Kentmore closed his eyes, forced a smile, and lifted his shoulders.

"Miss Hawick," he said, making Charlotte's heart squeeze with a sudden, sharp pain, fearing what his next words would be. "I cannot say what changes the future might bring. What I might say, however, is–"

"I am returned!" Lady Morton sailed into the room, just as Lord Kentmore placed his hand back upon her own, only to pull it away just as quickly. "Now, tell me, Lord Kentmore, have you been to a play recently? I have heard that there have been some marvelous productions of late, though I have not yet been so fortunate as to attend them."

Charlotte could do nothing other than listen to her mother speak, picking up her teacup and drinking what was left of it while Lord Kentmore answered in the most jovial voice, as though nothing of difficulty had been spoken between them. What Lord Kentmore had said had not brought her any sort of joy or reassurance. He had not said that yes, he wanted to be committed to her, desired to be a devoted husband who never again returned to the life of being a scoundrel. Instead, he had made a vague remark about the future and then had been forced to fall silent. Perhaps it was just as well he had not been permitted to say anymore, given the sorrow she already felt.

Why is my heart so foolish as to let itself warm to a gentleman who can never return my interest? Charlotte berated herself silently as her mother laughed at something Lord Kentmore said. *He cannot commit to a change in his life, he cannot promise to turn away from his roguish ways. And despite how much I might wish it, he cannot ever commit to me.*

~

CHARLOTTE MEANDERED through the garden of her father's townhouse, letting her fingers brush across the soft petals of the flowers there. She smiled to herself, only for a sudden thought to capture her attention.

Lord Kentmore.

The bouquet of flowers he had brought to her the previous day had been the first she had ever received from a gentleman and, as he had offered it to her, her heart had cried out – and even now, though she wanted to forget it, she could not. That cry had been one of affection, one of hope that it would be returned, though Charlotte was quite sure it would never be so. The more time she spent with him, the more she desired for him to be devoted solely to her, to turn his back entirely on such things, and yet, even now, he had not spoken to her of that. He had given her no assurance – so why did her heart continue to betray her with whispers of hope?

Sighing to herself, Charlotte continued through the garden, wondering at her own, tumultuous thoughts. She did not want to have her thoughts linger on Lord Kentmore, did not want to continue to consider all that she desired from him, for to do so would mean building up a hope that would, most likely, be shattered.

"Charlotte?"

She turned her head, seeing Lillian sitting on a bench near the scarlet roses.

"Lillian, I did not know you were here."

"I thought to come outside for a short while." Lillian held up The London Chronicle, a smile dancing about her lips. "I thought you might wish to see the poem that has been written within?"

Charlotte hesitated. Things had not been particularly warm between herself and her sister of late and though she had found herself thoroughly captured by the poems which had been printed in The London Chronicle, she did not desire to discuss them with her sister. Lillian had been enjoying Charlotte's close connection with Lord Kentmore in her own way, and had never enquired about how Charlotte felt at the prospect of marrying a rogue but had, instead, seemed to take great delight in it all. That had pushed Charlotte even further from her.

Evidently, her thoughts must have shown in her expression for Lillian's face fell and the paper was quickly settled in her lap.

"I have already read it," Charlotte said quickly. "That

is to say, Lord Kentmore read it to me earlier this afternoon."

Lillian nodded and looked away. "I know that you are displeased with me still," she said, her voice a little quiet. "Looking back, I mayhap ought not to have done as I did, but I think that it has turned out rather well, has it not?"

Charlotte stiffened.

"If you mean to say that Lord Glenfield has taken an interest in you, then yes, I suppose that it has."

Her sister tilted her head, saying nothing as she looked into Charlotte's eyes for a long moment.

"That has been a pleasant consequence, I will admit, though you must understand that there is also concern in my heart for you."

Closing her eyes, Charlotte shook her head.

"You have not asked me about my feelings ever since the news of my courtship ran around society."

"Because I was sure that you would soon realize just how wonderful this is to be for you!"

"Wonderful?"

Charlotte's voice cracked.

Lillian nodded, her eyes wide with enthusiasm.

"Yes, of course! You are to be a Marchioness! Your standing in society will be great and–"

"And I would give it all up for a gentleman who truly cared for me, Lillian!" Charlotte threw up her hands, her frustration boiling furiously, a sharpness there that had not been present before. "Despite my standing, even though I will be a Marchioness and, no doubt, have a good deal more coin than I have ever had before, I would give it all up to marry a gentleman who truly had an affection for me." She saw Lillian's eyes widen, saw the way that she opened her mouth, but Charlotte continued on regardless, her chest tight, her hands curling into fists. "The Marquess of Kentmore is a rogue. He states that though he will give that up for the time being, it will not be forever. What hope have I of a happy future? What hope have I of any sort of affection or true kindness or consideration between us? And what is worse, what if I, in my foolishness, find myself drawn to the very gentleman who could not care anything for me? Have you considered such things, Lillian? Or is money and standing all that matters to you?" She shook her head, seeing Lillian's face slowly beginning to drain of color. "I have never dreamed of love. I have never once imagined a marriage filled with affection and happiness, not until the possibility of that was taken from me. Now, the one thing I never thought to hope for is the *only* thing I long for, knowing I shall never gain it."

Lillian let out a small squeak, one hand reaching forward, one finger pointing – and Charlotte turned.

Lord Kentmore was standing only a few steps behind her, his eyes wide, his expression one of utter shock, the color pulling from his face. Charlotte gasped, stepping back from him, horrified about how much he would have overheard.

And then, without warning, he turned on his heel and strode away, leaving Charlotte staring after him in dismay.

CHAPTER FOURTEEN

I must go back.

Andrew hesitated as he made to climb up into his carriage. The conversation he had been about to have with Miss Hawick had been brought to a sudden end as Lady Morton had interrupted them both and Andrew had not had the opportunity to express to Miss Hawick his present considerations. She had asked him to give her the promise that he would remain entirely devoted to her for the rest of his days, that he would never again return to being a rogue, and though Andrew had not been able to give her what she desired, his intention had been to express to her the very great depths of confusion he found himself in at present. That, he had wanted to say, should give her the hope that he could alter himself entirely, and be just as she desired him to be.

Instead, he had been forced to keep those words back as Lady Morton had engaged him in conversation, and Andrew had seen the sadness lingering in Miss Hawick's eyes. She had offered very little to the rest of the conversation and had said nothing to him about their previous remarks. Now that he was to take his leave, Andrew found himself deeply frustrated.

"I do not want that sadness to linger," he muttered to himself, rubbing one hand over his eyes as his heart constricted, knowing just what she would think of him should he let the conversation be as it had been.

With a shake of his head, he turned away from the carriage.

"I will return in a few moments. I have forgotten something."

The coachman nodded, and Andrew made his way back into the house, still not quite certain what it was that he was going to say, but with his desire to express his heart burning within him. Being directed to the gardens, Andrew followed the butler to the door and then stepped outside, leaving the butler behind him.

"And I would give it all up for a gentleman who truly cared for me, Lillian!"

Miss Hawick threw up her hands, her voice tremulous, and Andrew's stomach clenched, his feet frozen in position. He could see Miss Hawick, and had been about to call out a greeting, but now, the sound of her voice and the words that she spoke tied him to his position, silencing his lips. Even if he tried to leave, even if he desired to turn about and leave this house, he did not think that his limbs would move, such was the heaviness settling within him. So he simply stood there as Miss Hawick went on, her words delivered with a passionate unhappiness.

"Despite my standing, despite the fact that I will be a

Marchioness and, no doubt, have a good deal more coin than I have ever had before, I would give it all up to marry a gentleman who truly had an affection for me."

Miss Hawick sniffed, though her words continued to rattle toward Andrew at a frantic pace. He knew that he ought to leave, ought to step away, given that she had no knowledge that he was here. But his heart demanded that he remain, insisted that he listen to every word, given that they were spoken with honesty – an honesty that he would never hear from her otherwise.

"The Marquess of Kentmore is a rogue."

Andrew dropped his head, the title he had once claimed with great delight and even pleasure now burning into his soul, offering him nothing but shame.

"He states that though he will give that up for the time being, it will not be forever. What hope have I of a happy future? What hope have I of any sort of affection or true kindness or consideration between us? And what is worse, what if I, in my foolishness, find myself drawn to the very gentleman who could not care anything for me? Have you considered such things, Lillian? Or is money and standing all that matters to you?"

And are stolen kisses, fleeting embraces, and words that hold no promise all that matters to me? Andrew closed his eyes, his stomach roiling. *What if all that I once held as important was never more than dirt and ashes?*

Miss Hawick's voice faltered, her hands in tight fists by her sides, and though Andrew could see that her sister knew of his presence, given the whiteness of her cheeks and her wide eyes which continued to stare at him, Miss Lillian said nothing. Clearly, Miss Charlotte Hawick had no knowledge of what had caused her sister's stillness, perhaps lost in her speech, given that it held so much emotion.

Andrew closed his eyes. *I am responsible for so much of her pain.*

Taking a breath, Miss Hawick put out her hands to either side and then dropped them back to her sides.

"I have never dreamed of love. I have never once imagined a marriage filled with affection and happiness, not until the possibility of that was taken from me. Now, the one thing I never thought to hope for is the *only* thing I long for, knowing I shall never gain it."

Miss Lillian Hawick, finally finding her voice, let out a small squeak and pointed directly at Andrew – and all strength seemed to leave his body. He could only stand and stare as Charlotte turned to face him, her eyes going wide as she took in his presence. She took a step back rather than moving towards him and, on seeing that, Andrew's strength returned to him.

He fled. Rather than go to her, rather than speak to her as he had intended, he turned and took his leave of the gardens and of her. Climbing back into the carriage, he rapped quickly on the roof and urged the coachman to make haste, a sense of relief writhing through him as he sat back and leaned his head against the squabs.

The carriage took him along the cobbled streets, the gentle rolling offering a comfort that Andrew could not reach.

I should have stayed.

The shame of his retreat was like a heavy weight on his shoulders, making his mortification complete. What sort of fellow was he to run from such a situation as this? He had never considered himself to be a coward, and yet, instead of walking towards her, instead of taking her hands in his and speaking to her as he had intended, he had run.

Leaning forward, Andrew put his elbows on his knees and dug his fingers into his hair, his face scalded with shame.

"I never expected to care for her with such strength," he muttered to himself, his eyes closing again. "I never thought that I would find myself in the least bit concerned about what she thought and felt."

But now I am overwhelmed by it.

Andrew lifted his head and sat back as the carriage turned towards his townhouse. His heart was heavy, his thoughts a swirling mass of confusion, and his fingers itched with the urge to write; to pour it all into the written word in the hope of finding the smallest sense of calm.

It was the only avenue he had, the only way he had to express all that he felt for, given his foolishness here, it was quite clear that he could never speak those words to Miss Hawick. Instead, he had to hope and pray that she would read his words in The London Chronicle and perhaps feel her heart soothed just a little.

All that matters to me now is her.

That thought struck Andrew hard and he sucked in a breath, his eyes flaring wide as he stared straight ahead, astonished by such a realization. What did it mean? How could he understand it? And why did the thought of returning to the life he had once lived now seem so dull and banal compared to being solely in her company?

~

Andrew's pen flew over the page, his quill scratching as he wrote and wrote and wrote. This time, it was not poetry that he wrote with the intention of sending it to The London Chronicle, but words that he prayed would empty his heart and mind of all that he felt, all that was tormenting him.

He could not free himself from it.

The door opened, but Andrew waved a hand, dismissing the servant.

"I am not to be disturbed."

"I was informed that you stated I could come in to call on you at any time."

Andrew looked up, seeing Lord Glenfield stroll into the room.

"Glenfield. Apologies, I am writing and–"

"I shall not disturb your focus for long. I came to fetch the mask for the ball tomorrow evening." His eyes twinkled as Andrew frowned. "The masquerade?"

"How could I forget?" Andrew muttered, finding no joy in the thought. Previously, he had been delighted about attending masquerades, for it was another opportunity for him to steal the attention of any lady he desired, heedless as to who they were, or what standing they held. They did not know who he was – not unless he revealed it to them, for he always wore an excellent mask that hid most of his face. How much he had enjoyed such things before! But now, there was a heaviness about it, as though he did not really wish to attend. "The mask, yes. I borrowed it from you for the last masquerade, did I not?"

Lord Glenfield nodded, and Andrew rang the bell, waiting for a footman to come to the room. Thereafter, he directed him to fetch the mask for Lord Glenfield and then picked up the sand to save his work.

"Is everything quite all right?"

Andrew sighed, put down his sander, and rose to his feet.

"No, it is not."

"And why not?"

Again, Andrew let out another sigh.

"It is because of this connection with Miss Hawick, this nearing betrothal, for I shall have to ask her very soon." He went to pour a brandy, recalling how he had come upon Miss Hawick earlier that day, declaring to her sister just how much she had lost in becoming tied to him, how much she now longed for love – the one thing that she was certain she could never find in him, in their connection. "I am uncertain."

"Uncertain?" Lord Glenfield tilted his head. "In what way?"

It was the first time that Andrew had been given an opportunity to put words to his feelings, and the thought was somewhat intimidating. He and Lord Glenfield had been friends for a very long time indeed, but given that they had both been nothing but rogues and rascals for that time. They had not often even considered discussing such things. He coughed, shrugging.

"It is... well, it is strange, that is all."

"What is strange?"

Andrew closed his eyes, fighting the desire to tell his friend that it was nothing and that he need not concern himself any more with it.

"Ever since I first met the lady, I have found myself frustrated with her lack of positive response to my work, to the published poems. The fact that she compared it with other writers, to the point of taking her friend to purchase a book on poetry, irritated me a great deal. Since that time, I have found myself eagerly desiring to impress my work upon her, to have her look favorably upon it."

Lord Glenfield's eyebrow lifted.

"Why does her opinion matter so much?"

"I could not tell you that because I do not understand it myself," Andrew replied, before taking a sip of his brandy. "On top of that, when this courtship began, I told her in no uncertain terms that I did not expect to give up my roguish ways entirely."

A frown crossed his friend's forehead.

"You said as much to me also."

"And I am well aware of your opinion of it." Andrew looked away briefly, aware that his tone had been a little sharp. "Forgive me, my friend. This is what has troubled me, I confess, and I am not doing particularly well when it comes to considering what to do next."

Lord Glenfield nodded, accepting Andrew's apology.

"I do not want to be wed." Andrew spoke firmly and clearly but yet felt himself aware that inwardly, he did not entirely believe what he said. "I have never wanted to marry and now, to be forced into that position has brought about a good deal of frustration on my part." He waved one hand. "Yes, I am aware that there is much that could be said about how that is my failing, but that is not my concern at present."

Lord Glenfield let out a small, rather heavy sigh.

"What is it, then?"

Andrew flung out his hands, his words coming more readily now.

"It is the unsettling realization that what she has asked of me – which is that I give up my interests entirely – is something that does not now seem as repugnant to me as it once did." He shook his head. "And I cannot explain the reason behind that. For heaven's sake, Glenfield, I had Lady Faustine come to find me in the gardens at that soiree and, when she tried to kiss me, I felt as though I might cast up my accounts! I pushed her back, I told her that I could never be to her, again, what I had previously been, and I strode away from her!"

"I am glad to hear it!"

Squeezing his eyes closed, Andrew let out a slow breath.

"But why am I doing such a thing? I have never said to Charlotte that I will turn to her and be devoted to her and yet, within myself, I find that desire growing, replacing all that I have once been and know!" Opening his eyes, he swallowed thickly. "I was going to tell her about my confusion earlier today, but her mother interrupted the conversation. Thereafter, I went to my carriage, only to find my heart demanding that I return and explain all to her. I... I did not want to have her under any illusion that I was still determined to do as I had previously said."

"I see." Lord Glenfield tilted his head. "And what did she say?"

Andrew blew out a long breath, raking one hand through his hair.

"She did not have the opportunity to listen to me. I was informed that she was in the garden with her sister and, upon making my way there, overheard her speak of all that she regretted in being joined to me, of how she had never hoped for love but now, in the awareness that she was to marry a rogue, realized just how much she desired such a thing. Of course, there was pain expressed that she would never have love offered to her either." Andrew dropped his head, a little ashamed. "You will think poorly of me – as I think poorly of myself – but I turned on my heel and took my leave. I did not know what to say."

Lord Glenfield blinked.

"Oh. And did she see you? Did she know that you were there?"

Andrew nodded.

"I am lost in a sea of tumult," he muttered, only for Lord Glenfield to begin to smile.

That smile spread to a grin and, as Andrew watched, confused at his friend's reaction, Lord Glenfield began to laugh. Andrew's astonishment grew all the more, only for him to then frown as, rather than give an explanation, Lord Glenfield continued to lose himself in mirth, evidently at Andrew's expense.

"Forgive me, my friend!" Lord Glenfield spoke,

perhaps seeing Andrew's discontentment. "I do not mean to be so foolish and indeed, it is not that I am laughing at you!"

Andrew scowled.

"Then why do you laugh?"

"Because," his friend grinned, sitting forward in his chair, "do you not realize *why* you desire to pull away from Lady Faustine and towards Miss Hawick instead? Do you not have any inkling as to why that might be?"

Blinking, Andrew scowled.

"I have just told you that I cannot understand it. Why, then, would you ask me such a thing? Is it not clear to you that I am struggling? I feel as though I have lost myself and do not know who I am any longer!"

Lord Glenfield's smile did not fade.

"My dear friend, I believe that you have had an interest – an *affection* – for Miss Hawick since the very moment you met her." Andrew's mouth dropped open. "You will tell me that I am foolish, of course, that I speak nothing but nonsense, but I can assure you, that desire you had for her to not only acknowledge your work, but appreciate it, came from a genuine interest in the lady herself."

Immediately, Andrew scoffed at this, shaking his head fervently.

"You are quite mistaken there, my friend. I thought nothing of the lady in that regard!"

"Are you quite certain?"

"She exasperated me by her remarks about my work!" Andrew exclaimed, as though this was all the explanation that his friend needed. "Her comparison of it to other works was maddening!"

"Why?"

Andrew flung out his hands.

"Because I wanted..." His hands fell to his sides as he fought to find an explanation that did not involve him accepting all that Lord Glenfield had said. "Because I wanted her to think as well of my work as she did of others," he said, slowly, his brow furrowing as he ran one hand over his chin.

"Which is rather strange, is it not?" Lord Glenfield lifted an eyebrow. "You had every other young lady in London sighing and cooing over your poetry, but you *also* had Miss Hawick speaking a little more frankly and considerately than they. Why, if you had so many of them delighting in what you had written, did you care so much about one young lady's thoughts?"

It was a question that Andrew could not answer. He frowned, hard, then threw back his brandy to delay offering Lord Glenfield an answer. This only made his friend chuckle all over again and Andrew's heart twisted, lost in a myriad of thoughts and feelings.

"I cannot have any real affection for her," he muttered, rubbing one hand over his eyes. "That is preposterous."

"Is it?" Lord Glenfield lifted his eyebrows. "I can tell you this, my friend, I have a genuine and growing affection for Miss Lillian Hawick – no, you need not look at me with such surprise – and with that comes a growing and steady desire to be the very best gentleman I can be. I am eager to know what she thinks, what she feels, what she delights in, and what she does not. I want to know everything about her and to spend as much time as I can in her company." He smiled, a light in his eyes that Andrew had never seen before. "That does not mean that I am not aware of her flaws and faults, just as she is aware of mine. I speak with too much flirtation at times, and I am inclined to tease - which she does not like, and she is inclined to be a little too fervent in her manner and speech at times, though I understand now why she is so." His smile softened. "If she thought poorly of me – or of something that I did, I should be greatly displeased, and would do my utmost to improve myself. Does that not speak to you, my friend? Can you not see that there is the same desire within you, when it comes to your poetry, *and* to your fight between turning back to your flirtations and the like, or turning away from them all?"

Andrew got up from his chair, feeling unsettled and restless.

"I do not think that your affections for Miss Lillian can be compared to my interest in Miss Charlotte."

"Why not?"

"Because it is not the same!"

His friend rose, came across to where Andrew stood, and poured himself a brandy, refilling Andrew's glass along with it.

"Then you must ask yourself what it is that you feel when it comes to the lady. You must discover *why* you have such an interest in her, why you desire to improve yourself so that she thinks better of your work... and of you yourself."

"She is to be my wife. Of course I do not want her to

always think poorly of me! Is that not reason enough?"

Lord Glenfield shrugged.

"You will not like my answer should I disagree with you, though I believe that you already know what it is."

Andrew scowled.

"I have no affection for her, no interest that is steadily growing. I–"

"Yes, you do." Lord Glenfield put a hand on Andrew's shoulder, looking back at him steadily. "You and I have been friends for many a year, and it would not be right of me to let this go without further conversation. My friend, you *do* have a growing and steady affection for the lady. You say that you are battling between the desire to return to your life as you have been living it for so long and the thought of giving it all up and remaining devoted to Miss Hawick. You have found yourself physically withdrawing from those who once held you spellbound, no doubt with a sense of guilt welling up within you at a single touch from Lady Faustine!" He chuckled as Andrew winced. "I can assure you that the only reason you have that fight is because your heart is affected, whether you wish to admit it to yourself or not." He lifted his hand, picked up his brandy, and smiled. "Now, I must return to my townhouse to prepare for the masquerade." Finishing his brandy, he set the glass down on the table and gave Andrew a nod. "Excuse me, my friend. I will see you again very soon."

Without giving Andrew the chance to respond, or the opportunity to argue against all that had been said, Lord Glenfield walked out of the room, leaving Andrew staring after him, his heart hammering furiously. Lord

Glenfield had stated things very clearly indeed, but Andrew still fought against it, the desire to accept the fact that he might well have an interest – more than that, an affection – for the lady seemed to approach him like a shadow that threatened to cover him completely. If he dared let himself believe it, then Andrew knew that every single thing in his life would change.

Dropping his head, Andrew pushed his fingers through his hair again, thinking back to how he had felt at the moment that he had come upon Miss Hawick in the garden. Had not his heart cried out? Had he not had the urge to sweep her up in his arms and confess that he no longer wanted to be a rogue, no longer desired attentions from any other than her?

And instead, he had stepped back, silencing himself, and hastened back to his carriage.

I have been a coward and a fool.

Making his way slowly back towards his writing desk, Andrew sat down again and picked up his quill. The words came more cautiously this time, but they came nonetheless until, finally, Andrew had his answer to the questions filling his heart.

CHAPTER FIFTEEN

"I do not feel as though this mask is adequate enough, Mama."

Charlotte said nothing, looking away as her sister fussed with the ribbons of the mask. Ever since the previous afternoon, she had lost herself in a pool of sorrow, embarrassment, and upset, made all the worse by the knowledge that Lord Kentmore had left the gardens the moment that she had looked at him, and had chosen, thereafter, neither to write to her nor come to call. She could not imagine what it was that he had thought upon hearing her speech. She could not bring herself to consider what he had thought of her statement about him. She had said so many things and yes, all of them were quite true, but all the same, she could not imagine what it was that he had felt in hearing her say them all so bluntly.

"Are you quite well, Charlotte?"

A little surprised, Charlotte looked at her mother as

they waited in line to greet the host of the masquerade ball.

"Yes, Mama."

"You have been rather quiet the last two days."

Charlotte offered a vague smile.

"I have had something weighing on my mind, Mama, that is all."

Lady Morton leaned closer to her.

"Might it be that Lord Kentmore is the one you think on? I have noticed his attentions to you becoming a little more determined, my dear."

"I am sure that Lord Kentmore wishes to propose," Lillian interjected, making Charlotte look at her sharply, though most of her expression was hidden from her sister, given the mask she was wearing. "And once he does, I think that Lord Glenfield shall also."

"Lillian!" Their mother's voice was a low hiss as she took hold of Lillian's arm and pulled her closer. "Do keep your voice down! There are many nearby who would like nothing more than to whisper about all that you have said. Please, be a good deal more considered in your speech, whether it be true or not."

"But it *is* true," Lillian protested, albeit in a much quieter voice. "Lord Glenfield has told me as much, though he has not yet spoken to Father. I know that he means to do so very soon."

"Once Lord Kentmore has proposed?" Lady Morton whispered, sending a look towards Charlotte which made her tremble inwardly. "Then that must mean that he desires very much to betrothe himself to you, Charlotte! Has he made any indication of that as yet?"

Charlotte did not know what to say. Ought she to state that yes, she knew of Lord Kentmore's intentions, even though it had not been spoken of between them as yet, or should she remain silent on the matter?

Her mother squeezed her hand.

"I shall not press you, my dear. I can see that there is something on your mind, but you do not wish to speak of it as yet. That is understandable. What passes between a gentleman and a lady he is courting ought, sometimes, to stay private. Though," she continued, a bright smile spreading across her face, "if that is to be as your sister hopes, then I do hope that you will accept, Charlotte?"

"Of course I shall, Mama," Charlotte answered, a little dully. "I have no reason not to."

Her mother beamed at her, but there was no time for them to say anything more. Instead, they greeted their hosts and stepped into the ballroom, and Charlotte caught her breath at the beauty of it. There were garlands and wreaths of white roses and laurel leaves positioned all around the room, the many candelabras making the walls appear as though they were burnished gold. There were mirrors on every wall, interspersed with pieces of magnificent art, and the floor itself bore a chalked piece of art, which, from where Charlotte stood, looked to be more roses and laurel leaves, to match the arrangements on the walls. Despite her own inner turmoil, Charlotte could not help but smile at the beauty of it, at the splendor that lifted her spirits from the doldrums.

"Good evening to you all!" It was Lord Glenfield's jovial voice that made Charlotte recognize him immediately, even with the mask that covered both of his eyes and a good deal of his forehead. "How splendid to see you here this evening. Is not this ball truly magnificent?"

He beamed at them all and Charlotte could not help but smile at his enthusiasm.

"But how did you know that this was Lillian?" Lady Morton asked as Lord Glenfield chuckled.

"Ah, because she informed me of the very mask that she was to wear, and told me that there would be a single peacock feather to the right of her head," Lord Glenfield said, as Lady Morton smiled. "Now, Miss Hawick, might I ask you to dance? Given that we cannot use dance cards this evening, I believe I shall try my luck and steal more than one dance from you, if I am permitted?"

His gaze went to Lady Morton, who smiled and nodded, clearly delighted with the prospect of having both daughters wed very soon. Charlotte, however, sighed softly as she watched her sister take her leave with Lord Glenfield, seeing the bright smile on Lillian's face, and knowing that it came from a heart that was full simply because of being in Lord Glenfield's company.

Would that I could have the same.

"My dear?" Lady Morton touched Charlotte's arm. "What is it that troubles you so?"

Charlotte shook her head, trying to smile.

"It is nothing, Mama."

"Tell me the truth." Lady Morton's expression softened. "I know that you think of Lord Kentmore. I have not pressed you on the matter, but you must be truthful with me, my dear. It is the only thing that will bring you relief from whatever it is that you have been contemplating for so long."

Releasing a long breath, Charlotte turned her gaze to her mother.

"I have... feelings for Lord Kentmore which are not returned."

Her mother's smile became fixed in place.

"What do you mean, they are not returned?"

"That is what I mean." Charlotte let out a slow breath, closing her eyes for a moment. "Mama, I have not told him of my affection, and I dare not even admit it to myself, for fear of the injury which will follow."

"Injury?" Her mother frowned gently. "Why should you be injured?"

"Because," Charlotte replied, tears catching in her throat, "as I have just now told you, he does not return my affections."

Her mother tilted her head.

"Why would you say such a thing as that? What is it about him that makes you believe that there is no interest there?"

A little confused, Charlotte took a moment before she answered.

"Because he has not said any such thing to me."

"But you have not said anything either," her mother replied, making Charlotte's brows furrow. "You have not told him of your interest, you have not said a word to him, but now you are concerned that he does not feel anything akin to your own heart? How can you be sure if you have not asked him?"

Charlotte closed her eyes.

"Because he is a rogue, Mama."

"No, he *was* a rogue," her mother insisted, albeit in a

tender manner. "I have seen him as he has been in your company, I have watched as a tenderness has grown in his gaze as he watches you." She smiled and took Charlotte's hand again. "Do not lose heart, my dear. Urge yourself to speak the truth to him, and you may be surprised by just how much is returned to you."

Listening carefully, Charlotte took a slow breath and then let it out again, hardly daring to believe that anything her mother had said was true. Had there really been a tenderness in Lord Kentmore's expression towards her, or had her mother simply been mistaken?

"Now, why do you not take a few minutes to compose yourself and then return to me?" Lady Morton shrugged lightly. "No one will know who you are, so it will not matter if you take a short while at the side of the ballroom to regain yourself. I will stay here."

Charlotte nodded, not trusting her voice as a wave of emotion crashed down over her. Making her way to the side of the ballroom, where the shadows hid her a little more, she took off her mask, pulled out her handkerchief, and wiped her eyes delicately.

I am falling in love with a rogue, she thought to herself, her tears beginning to burn afresh, though Charlotte did her best to keep them back. *I do not know if I can dare permit myself to believe what my mother has said.* A sense of joy began to fill her, forcing her tears away and instead, replacing them with a small smile. *But if there is hope, then that changes everything.*

"Miss Hawick, is it?"

Charlotte lifted her head, pushing her handkerchief back into her pocket.

"Yes, it is I, though with my mask off, I am certain anyone would be able to recognize me." She searched the face of the lady in front of her, but the mask was much too ornate, the feathers too many to make it clear. "Forgive me, I do not know who you are and–"

"That is not important. What *is* important is that you end your courtship with Lord Kentmore."

A sudden whoosh of breath rushed out of Charlotte, leaving her feeling a little weak and off-balance.

"I – I beg your pardon?"

"I know that this courtship is nothing but a falsehood. Lord Kentmore has spoken to me only recently and informed me of his disappointment and frustration in being so caught up in a match that he has no real interest in. I am sure that you must feel the same, though mayhap part of you is pleased that you are connected to a Marquess?"

Charlotte swallowed tightly, lifting her chin.

"I do not have any need to explain myself to you." The words the lady had spoken ran right through her, however, wrapping around her like barbed thorns. "Now, if you will excuse me, I–"

"No one else in London is aware of what happened," the lady interrupted, coming to stand a little closer to Charlotte. "There have been no whispers, no rumors of any sort, have there? So why, then, would you insist upon your courtship? He is a gentleman with a particular... way of living, is he not?" Her eyes glittered behind her mask, making Charlotte's stomach twist. "He spoke to me only a few days ago, when we stood *alone* together in the gardens. We spoke intimately, you understand, and I heard him say very clearly that he had no interest in marrying, how he wished he was free of it, how he wished he was free of *you*."

Pain seared Charlotte's heart, and her eyes began to flood with tears, all hope fading away.

"You have the power to end this ridiculous courtship before it turns into something that you *cannot* step back from," the lady continued, sniffing lightly as though Charlotte ought to recognize that she spoke nothing but sense. "It is your own foolishness which makes you linger, is it not? Why would you tie yourself to such a gentleman when you know the very sort of character that he is?"

Closing her eyes, Charlotte tried to steady herself.

"There is no saying what the future might bring," she said hoarsely, echoing Lord Kentmore's words, only for the lady to laugh aloud and so harshly that it made her wince.

"As though a rogue would change," she laughed, as tears began to fall to Charlotte's cheeks. "You are not speaking sense! You know as well as I that any scoundrel will remain just as he is, no matter *who* he is connected with. They will speak kind words, gentle words, even sweet words to you, but none of them hold truth. Given that I shared a kiss with him very recently, it makes it quite plain to me that he will never commit himself to you - which is, I presume, what you were hoping for?"

It was as though her heart had been ripped from her chest. Charlotte could barely breathe, her hands gripping together as dizziness overwhelmed her.

"Ah, Miss Hawick, there you are. Your mother said... oh, excuse me."

Charlotte's vision blurred as she looked straight at the gentleman who had come to greet her, recognizing Lord Kentmore's voice.

"I – I was..."

"Miss Hawick was just coming to the realization that she wanted to end your courtship," the lady said, her words firm and decisive.

"End our courtship?" Lord Kentmore did not sound pleased, as Charlotte had expected, shock filling his voice and his expression as he reached up to take off his mask. "Whatever can you mean, Charlotte? Why would you do such a thing?"

"Because she knows that you are a rogue and that you are not inclined towards marriage," the lady said again, as Charlotte fought to find enough strength to answer. "Given what *we* have shared of late, it makes sense for her to bring it to an end. After all no one from society thinks that there has been anything untoward happen, so why should you continue towards matrimony? There is no reason for it."

There came a short silence and, as Charlotte blinked to clear her vision, she saw Lord Kentmore take a step towards the lady, his shoulders lifted, his head lowered but his face flushing.

"What we *shared*?" he repeated, his anger evident in every syllable, his voice rasping. "I hardly think–"

"It is probably for the best." Charlotte closed her eyes tightly, swaying slightly as she spoke. "I understand now. I should never have believed that there was any hope of a future where you thought only of me." Her voice broke, tears beginning to dust her lashes again. "Excuse me."

She turned to leave, only for Lord Kentmore to catch her hand.

"Charlotte, wait, please! This is not as it sounds. I—"

Shaking her head, Charlotte pulled her hand away and, without another word, without so much as another glance towards him, hurried away. She did not even look where she was going, her vision clouded with her tears. Finding herself outside, she put one hand on the doorframe and breathed in great gasps of cold air.

"Miss Hawick?"

She dared not look up for fear it was Lord Kentmore.

"It is Lord Glenfield. Are you quite all right? I came out for a breath of air after my dance and…" He leaned closer to her, then caught his breath. "Goodness, you are not all right, are you? What can I do?"

Charlotte shook her head, her handkerchief already sodden.

"I just want to go home."

"Then take my carriage." Lord Glenfield leaned towards a nearby footman and directed him sharply, before returning to Charlotte's side. "It will be here in a moment. Shall I fetch your mother or sister?"

"No, please do not." Her words punctuated by sobs, she shook her head again, not able to look at him. "Just inform them that I have a headache and choose to return home. I have made that excuse before, and it has been accepted."

Lord Glenfield put a hand to her arm for a moment, though Charlotte knew it was meant only as a kind gesture.

"Is this because of Lord Kentmore?"

Charlotte looked up at him. There was understanding in his eyes and Charlotte could not help but nod, not trusting herself to speak anything more.

"Then I will talk to him, will berate him for whatever it is that he has done," came the reply, just as the carriage drew up. "I do wish you well, Miss Hawick. Lord Kentmore is not worthy of you, not worthy in the least."

There was no strength within her to reply, though she did accept his arm and permitted him to help her up into the carriage. Whispering a thank you, she closed her eyes again and leaned her head back, more than ready to make her way home and as far from Lord Kentmore as she could.

"My courtship is at an end," she whispered, brokenly. Her heart cried out as she spoke those words, telling her that she did not want such a thing to have happened. She did not want to have separated from the gentleman who had begun to steal her heart but, at the same time, recognized that she would never be happy should she remain with him. Her tears began to flow in earnest and Charlotte let them fall, finally giving in to all of her sorrow and pain, her heart broken beyond repair.

CHAPTER SIXTEEN

"What did you do?"

Andrew blinked as a strong hand grasped his arm and flung him around, his feet unsteady. "Glenfield, whatever is the meaning of this?"

"I have just had to lead Miss Hawick into my carriage so that she might return home, seeing her broken-hearted and sorrowful," his friend hissed, his eyes narrowing. "I know that you are responsible. Whatever did you do to her?"

Andrew's heart tore and he pulled the mask from his face so he might see his friend clearly.

"That is what I have been trying to discover. I did not think that Charlotte would leave, however." He swallowed tightly, gesturing to Lady Faustine. "Evidently, Lady Faustine thought to inform Charlotte that I am just as much a rogue as I have ever been, and that she has no hope of ever having me fully devoted to her."

"But that is quite true!" Lady Faustine exclaimed, throwing up her hands. "I do not understand what the trouble is! I have done just as I thought was best, seeing that you were pushing me away, declaring that such a thing could never be again… well, I recognized that it came from a strange thought that you had to be loyal to this young lady! Now, you are free."

"I do not *wish* to be free!" Andrew answered, speaking to her with as much force as he dared. "Miss Faustine, do you not understand? I have no interest in furthering my connection with you, whether I am courting Miss Hawick or not. I have no interest in pursuing anything any longer, aside from her!"

"Miss Hawick clearly did not understand that," Lord Glenfield muttered, darkly. "Why did you not say such things to her?"

Andrew spread out his hands.

"I had no opportunity." He made to step away from them both, the urge to go after her burning through him. "But I must speak to her, I must make her understand–"

"I informed her that we shared a kiss."

Ice formed over Andrew's heart as he turned back slowly towards Lady Faustine, seeing how her eyes gleamed behind her mask.

"I beg your pardon?"

"I told her that we shared a kiss," the lady repeated, shifting her stance slightly so that she stood tall. "That is true, is it not? I wanted her to understand that any hope she had of having your full attention was not to be continued."

Fear loomed, its shadow falling over Andrew entirely.

"We did not share a kiss," he said, as quietly but as

firmly as he could. "Lord Glenfield, you recall that I told you about this?"

Much to his relief, his friend nodded.

"I do," came the answer. "I recall that you told me how much you disliked Lady Faustine's nearness to you, that you stepped away when she attempted to kiss you."

"Precisely." Andrew looked back at Lady Faustine, angry with her for what she had done in pushing Miss Hawick away, but all the more furious with himself. Had he not run from Miss Hawick the previous day, had he had the strength of heart and mind to go to her, to confess all that he felt – albeit some confusion with it – then she might never have listened to Lady Faustine. "You tried to kiss me, Lady Faustine, and I pushed you back, I tore myself from you with a fervor that I have never before experienced. I told you, in no uncertain terms, that the thought of ever being in your company again in that way practically repulsed me – and yet, you took that as a promise from me that I would return to you, should my courtship come to an end?"

Lady Faustine blinked.

"A kiss from my lips *repulsed* you?"

Andrew did not hold himself back; he did not choose kinder words for the lady's sake. Instead, he spoke fervently, wanting to make it perfectly clear to her all that he was saying.

"I do not want to be a rogue any longer. All that you have said to Miss Hawick is patently false. I have been lost in confusion, I will admit, wondering why I begin to desire her company more than any other, why my heart quails at the thought of being apart from her – only for me to realize that the reason is Miss Hawick herself! She is the one who has changed my heart in a way that no one else has ever been able to."

"Then..." Lady Faustine took a step back from him, her expression still half hidden by her mask. "Do you mean to say that you intend to be as devoted to her as she desires you to be?"

It was as though a great and heavy cloud lifted from him. The confusion, the regret, the doubt and the struggle all faded away to give him perfect clarity.

He lifted his chin and set his shoulders.

"Yes," he said, as Lady Faustine gasped in shock. "You may think of me as a scoundrel and a rogue, but I am neither any longer. From this day forward, I declare that I shall never again return to such a way of life. Instead, my only thought shall be for Miss Hawick."

Lady Faustine blinked furiously, but she turned and hurried away before anything more could be said. Andrew let out a breath, his shoulders dropping as something like relief washed through him, making him realize just how much stress he had been carrying.

"You are a little late with your declaration, my friend."

Turning to look at Lord Glenfield, Andrew shook his head to himself.

"Yes, I can see that. How foolish I have been!" A heaviness settled on his shoulders, taking away some of the relief he had felt. "You told me the truth of my heart clearly and still, I pushed it away, and swam in the sea of confusion."

"But you have come to see it for yourself now, have you not? That is all that matters."

"What shall I do now?" Panic began to fill Andrew's heart. "If she is gone, if she means all that she says, then I am to be separated from her! Our courtship will be at an end and–"

"Her father is here, is he not?"

Andrew blinked, a little confused.

"Make it clear to him your intentions. That way, even if he returns home and hears the lady state that the courtship has come to an end, he will be able to make your intentions clear to her," Lord Glenfield suggested. "Yes, that might bring some confusion, but it will give you time to speak with her, to make your heart known to her."

Understanding and seeing the wisdom in that suggestion, Andrew nodded slowly.

"Then you think that I should not go to speak with her tonight?"

Lord Glenfield winced.

"Do you truly believe that would be wise? Given your reputation – which I know you now shun – can you really think it a good idea to go to Lord Morton's townhouse and speak with her, alone?"

Andrew's shoulders dropped.

"No, I do not think it would be."

"Then you should not."

Closing his eyes, Andrew scrubbed one hand over his face, his mask dangling from his other hand.

"What if she will not speak with me?" he asked, the fear of that beginning to rush through his veins, quickening his heart. "What if she believes all that Lady Faustine said to her and will not even tolerate the sight of me?"

Much to his surprise, Lord Glenfield grinned, his smile big and bright. "There is one way that you might pursue."

"Then tell me!" Andrew exclaimed at once. "What is it that you are thinking of?"

"Your poetry."

It was as though the air had been pulled from him as Andrew's delight began to shrink, shaking his head fervently. "No, I cannot do such a thing as that."

"You must. You know very well that she has been most impressed by the most recent of your work. Why do you not write to her that way? Confess all that you need to and this time, put your name to it. Let her see that *you* have been the writer all along and that it is because of her that the poems have altered so significantly."

Andrew's heart turned over on itself.

"You recognized that?"

His friend chuckled.

"Of course I did take note of the changes – and I recognized that it is because of her! You have begun to feel things that you have never experienced before, finding a depth in your connection, an intimacy there that, mayhap, you were always looking for but never realized." His smile softened. "The reason I can speak so is because that is what I feel with respect to Miss Lillian."

"I was not aware of it until now, the depths of my feelings." Hearing himself, Andrew scowled. "What I mean to say is that I did not permit myself to acknowledge it. I saw it, I felt it all, growing slowly, but with intention, and I withdrew from it... until I could withdraw no more."

"Then tell her that," came his friend's reply. "Tell her in your words as best you can and I am certain, all will turn out well."

EPILOGUE

"Have you seen this?"

Charlotte, her eyes sore from the weeping she had endured throughout the night, turned her attention away from the paper that Lillian held out to her.

"I am in no mood to read about society gossip, Lillian."

"It is not society gossip!" her sister exclaimed, her voice holding an excitement that made Charlotte frown. "It is more of those poems."

This did not lift Charlotte's spirits in the least.

"I have no interest in them, Lillian. Please, as I told you last evening, I had a severe headache and still find myself rather fatigued."

She had not yet informed her father and mother that she had ended the courtship between herself and Lord Kentmore, though it was still early enough in the day for that to take place. There was not enough strength within her to speak of it to them, not as yet, but that was her intention, at least. Her heart still tore with pain whenever she thought of it, her sorrow overwhelming, but the decision had been made, nonetheless. It was the right thing for her to do, she had told herself over and over again, hating that her heart still yearned for him, still wanted to cling to him, despite all that he had done, and all that he could never be to her.

"I think that you should read these." Lillian, refusing to accept Charlotte's disinterest, thrust the paper into her lap. "You must."

Charlotte wanted to throw the paper away, to demand that her sister leave her be. She wanted to scream that just because Lillian was happy and contented did not mean that she could simply force Charlotte to do whatever she pleased. Biting her tongue, she closed her eyes and shook her head.

"Please, Charlotte." Lillian's voice was softer now. "I am not suggesting it because of any other reason than that I know it will bring you joy."

"Joy?" Charlotte repeated, her chest tightening. "There can be no joy for me at this moment. Lillian, I beg of you, listen to me when I say that I cannot bear to read such a thing."

Her sister came to sit next to her rather than moving away, her eyes searching Charlotte's face.

"My dear Charlotte, I am well aware that there has been some difficulty between yourself and Lord Kentmore. Mayhap I was wrong to insist that you court and then become betrothed, given that my reasons were somewhat selfish, but all the same, I am glad to know that there has been happiness come out of it."

Confused as to what her sister meant, Charlotte looked away.

"I do not feel any happiness."

"You shall soon enough! Lord Kentmore spoke to our father last night."

Whipping her head around, Charlotte snatched in a breath, gazing at her sister with wide eyes.

"I beg your pardon?"

"I was there! For the moment Lord Kentmore stepped away, Lord Glenfield spoke with him thereafter! Our father had to give his consent twice within the space of a few minutes!"

Charlotte blinked, struggling to understand what her sister was saying. She had ended her connection to the Marquess of Kentmore last evening, so why had he then gone on to speak to her father, to seek his permission for them to wed? After all that had been said last evening by Lady Faustine, she had thought that he would feel nothing but relief at the ending of their courtship.

"Here." Charlotte felt the paper being pressed into her hands and, reluctantly, took it from her sister. "Now read it, my dear sister. It will lift your heart, I promise you."

Still a little unwilling, Charlotte turned her gaze to the page that Lillian had pushed her to read – and snatched in a breath.

Not only one but two pages were filled with poems. She counted twelve of them, some long, some short, but all of them filling up the entire space of each page.

"Goodness," she breathed, turning her attention to the first. "I must say, I was not expecting that."

Her sister giggled.

"I am sure that there is even more you will not expect."

Unsure as to what her sister meant in that regard, Charlotte began to read – and by the end of the first poem, found tears in her eyes. There was such raw emotion in each and every line. She could feel all that the writer expressed. The tumult, the confusion, the way that he had been torn this way and that... she could sense his desperation, his doubt, and his fear.

"Whoever this is, his writing has become significantly improved," she whispered, half to herself, before going to the next one.

Quite how long it took her to read them, Charlotte could not say. She took in each line, each word, with great consideration, her eyes filling with tears on occasion, her lips curving into a smile thereafter.

And then she reached the very last one.

Reading it slowly, her heart began to pound as she searched her way through every line. There was a sense of familiarity here, something that she could understand without being fully aware of what it was. Frowning hard, she made her way back to the beginning of it again, letting it sink into her very soul.

'The whispers of malice, the murmurs of deceit,
Are brought to you, unexpected and unwarranted.
A mask of lies, covered and garish,
Threatening to shake the ground where you stand.
Your hand is pulled from mine,
Darkness and shadow haunting your steps.
I cry out for you, but my voice is lost,

*The words spoken bring you naught but despair.
Oh, but if you would give me but a moment,
Then I might repair the brokenness.
Cast out the lies, my love, tread on them until they break!
Find my heart, no longer lost
But instead,
Only
Yours.'*

"Look." Lillian put out one finger, pointing to a line that Charlotte had not yet read. "Do you not see?"

It took Charlotte a moment to understand what her sister was saying, a second or two to take in what was written there but, the moment she took it in, it was as though the world shifted under her feet.

Lord Kentmore?

"It is your betrothed," Lillian murmured, one hand going to Charlotte's shoulder. "*He* has been the one writing all of these poems, I am sure of it! Right from the very beginning, he was the one who penned those poems, and now he has revealed it to all of society! Though, I believe that these poems are all for you. Some are about you - and you can see the tenderness and the sweetness in his words!"

"This... this cannot be," Charlotte whispered, her eyes fixing themselves on the page. "I would have known... I would have found out..."

"Evidently, you did not." Lillian pressed Charlotte's arm. "My dear sister, the gentleman cares for you a great deal! Is it not evident? Though there is obviously a good deal of confusion within him – or there was, at least, for these poems read like a story."

"Yes, they do," Charlotte agreed, her voice rasping with emotion. "He is confused, doubting his own feelings, uncertain of why he is desirous of turning his back on all that he once knew. Then, there is a path towards realization, towards understanding that his own heart has changed and the hope for a new beginning, a future reconsidered... only for the poem at the end to bring an end to that hope."

"What happened last evening?" Lillian asked, quietly, as Charlotte shook her head. "What lies is he speaking of?"

Charlotte closed her eyes as tears welled up in an instant.

"The very worst, though I believed every word." A hoarse laugh broke from her. "Though now I find that I am greatly troubled and confused myself, uncertain as to what all of this might mean! What was truth and what was a lie?"

Her sister smiled.

"You will have to ask him."

"I shall, I–"

"Miss Marshall has come to call."

The butler opened the door and Miss Marshall rushed in, her face pink and her hand holding The London Chronicle.

"My dear Charlotte, did you see this? Have you read them all? I confess that I have been both astonished and left in awe at the skill he has in writing such beautiful words!"

Charlotte rose to her feet, leaving the paper behind but grasping Miss Marshall's hand instead.

"Might you come out for a walk with me?"

Miss Marshall blinked.

"A walk?"

"Yes. I have somewhere that I must go, and I cannot have my mother or father with me."

Understanding drew itself into Miss Marshall's expression at once.

"Oh, of course. I would be glad to do so."

"Lillian, might you tell Mama that I have taken a short drive in the carriage with Miss Marshall?" Feeling a little frantic, Charlotte grasped her sister's hand. "Will you?"

Lillian placed her other hand on top of Charlotte's, calming her a little.

"I shall. I do hope that you will return to this house happier than you have ever been."

Charlotte smiled, though a tear slid down her cheek all the same.

"I thank you," she whispered, pausing for a moment to embrace her sister. "Thank you for practically forcing me to read those poems, Lillian, and for insisting that I wed Lord Kentmore in the first place! I did not think it at the time, did not believe it for many a day, but now, finally, I believe that I shall have the chance of both love and happiness, and my heart is filled with hope at that thought."

"Then go." Lillian urged her from the room, with Miss Marshall letting out an excited giggle. "You cannot wait a single moment!"

No, I cannot, Charlotte thought to herself, barely stopping to take her bonnet and gloves. *I must speak with him, I must talk with him about it all... and be truthful with him about the state of my heart.*

～

"Lord Kentmore."

A little breathless, Charlotte walked into his study, the door left open, and Miss Marshall stationed in the hallway, though Charlotte had every belief that she would make her way from one end of the hallway to the other rather than lingering near the door in the hope of hearing every word.

"Charlotte." Lord Kentmore's voice was breathless as he rose from his study chair, moving so quickly that it scraped back on the floor. "You... you are here. I..." Seemingly a little flustered, he pushed one hand through his hair, then gestured to a chair. "Please, do come and sit down. I–"

"I read your poems."

Lord Kentmore came towards her, rounding his desk as though he could not get to her fast enough.

"You did?"

"You wrote them all?" Charlotte's voice was thick with tears, though she smiled as he nodded, putting one hand to her heart. "That is why you were always so angry with me when I did not think too highly of them."

Lord Kentmore winced, closing his eyes briefly as he stopped only a step or two away from her. "It was my arrogance, I confess. Though, thereafter, I found that my desire to please you was not solely because of my own sense of self-importance. Rather, I wanted you to think well of my work so that you felt happy, contented, delighted, satisfied, or even joyous in what you read. It was your happiness and contentment I found myself seeking, rather than thinking of myself – and even that unsettled me!" He took a small step closer to her, his hands going out either side of him as he shook his head. "I have broken your heart, Charlotte, and for that I cannot apologize enough. I have reveled in idiocy, losing myself in confusion, unwilling to give myself up to all that I felt, simply because I did not want to. I did not want to lose the rogue. I did not want to step into a future that was different from the one I had hoped for... and yet, when I finally realized just how much of a fool I had been, you had stepped away from me."

A knot tied itself in Charlotte's stomach as she took a deep breath, knowing that there was one question she had to have the answer to.

"That lady who spoke to me–"

"Lady Faustine."

"Lady Faustine." Charlotte pressed her lips tightly together for a moment. "Did you share a kiss with her?"

The moment that Lord Kentmore shook his head, Charlotte went weak with relief, dropping her head forward and letting out a prolonged sigh.

"She tried to press her lips to mine." Lord Kentmore's voice was low, and when she looked at him, the colors in his eyes seemed to grow all the more intense. "It was at that moment, that *very* moment, that I realized that my heart was changed. Normally, in the past, I would have wrapped my arms around her and reveled in the connection but instead, I felt sick at the thought of doing so. I wanted nothing more to do with her – or with any other – and I confess that I told her as much." A tiny, rueful smile crept up one side of his mouth. "Then, when you asked me that day in your drawing room if I would be devoted to you, I did not give you a clear answer, though I found myself desiring to. I wanted to confess to you the waves of confusion and doubt that I had been captured by."

"And that is why you came back to the garden," Charlotte breathed, finding herself moving closer to him without having had any real intention of doing so. "You wanted to speak more with me."

He nodded.

"And instead, I heard you speaking of me in such an honest way that my heart quite broke. I saw then the pain and the sorrow that I had caused you and, within myself, came that strong determination never to do that again. I went home rather than speak with you and for that, I am truly sorry." His eyes squeezed closed for a moment. "I should have come closer to you, rather than run. Instead of lingering, I returned home, I sat at my writing desk, and I wrote and wrote and wrote – and then Lord Glenfield came in." A quiet chuckle came from his lips. "He told me the truth, which I refused to accept at first. Once I saw that he was right, I was determined to find you, to explain everything... only Lady Faustine got to you first." Reaching out, he took her hand in his and Charlotte moved closer still, not resisting him for even a moment. "I cannot tell you how sorry I am over all that I have done and all that you have had to endure."

Charlotte swallowed hard, smiling gently back at him, aware of the tears that were just behind her eyes.

"You have come to the truth at last," she whispered, as Lord Kentmore nodded fervently. "I saw the story in your poems, I followed the path that your heart has taken."

"And it is a path which has led me to you," he answered, his other hand going to find hers. "I do not deserve to have you beside me, Charlotte. I have known that from the very beginning of our connection, I am not worthy of you, given how beautiful, delightful, and affectionate you are, and how much of a scoundrel I have been."

"But that does not matter to me," Charlotte answered quickly, taking her hand from his and boldly, settling it upon his chest. "If you are true in your words, then you have turned your back upon all of that, have you not? You are going to be just as devoted to me as I am to you."

Lord Kentmore nodded slowly and then, with his free hand, lifted it so that it rested against her cheek. His eyes searched hers, the gold flecks within them transfixing her, just as they had always done.

"I am devoted to you, Charlotte." There was a quietness about his words, a tenderness which held a firmness with it. "I shall never turn my back on you, *never*. I will not go back to being a rogue but instead, I shall give you all of myself – my whole heart – and live a life of utter devotion to you."

A single tear fell from Charlotte's cheek as she looked back at him, with Lord Kentmore brushing it away gently with his thumb, making her smile softly.

"Kentmore." Her eyes fluttered closed for a moment, her emotions welling up within her, crying out for her to speak. "My dear Kentmore, I have been torn asunder knowing that my heart has filled itself with an affection for you which I feared would never be returned." Opening her eyes, she snatched in a breath as Lord Kentmore began to lower his head, a whisper of anticipation climbing up her spine. "I told myself I was a fool for falling in love with a rogue – even if he was to be my husband – but now I can say I am a fool no longer."

A small hint of a smile danced across his lips.

"You could never be a fool, Charlotte," he murmured, his other hand tugging away from hers but only then to wrap his arm about her waist so that she was caught up against him. "I am the fool, I assure you, who has been given more than he ever deserved."

When he lowered his head, Charlotte was ready for him. Her lips met his, her hands slid up around his shoulders, her fingers brushing the hair at the nape of his neck. This kiss, however, was nothing like their first. There was no desperate, furious passion but instead, a sweetness, a tenderness which gently called to her. It was as though he were kissing her for the first time, as though he had never done such a thing before.

"My goodness." Lord Kentmore breathed softly against her lips, his forehead resting against hers. "I have never kissed a lady that I am in love with before." Another breath whispered across her cheeks. "My darling, it is more wonderful, more beautiful than anything I have ever experienced."

Charlotte leaned her head against his shoulder,

pulling herself all the more into his embrace, her heart so happy, it was overflowing with sheer joy.

"We have found our path together, it seems," she murmured, tilting her head up so that his lips came near hers again. "Our love will lead us into a happy future, I am sure of it."

He kissed her lightly but did not linger.

"As am I. You will marry me, Charlotte?"

Charlotte smiled up at him, marveling at just how wonderful this moment felt.

"Of course I shall... on one condition."

Lord Kentmore pulled back just a little, his expression suddenly grave.

"Name it."

Her hand brushed against his cheek, a soft smile on her lips.

"Promise me that you will write poetry for me still, my love. I have come to love your words, and I desire to read much, much more of them."

A brilliant smile spread across Lord Kentmore's face as he clasped her to himself once more.

"I shall write it every day," he promised, coming to kiss her again. "And I shall write it solely for you."

I LOVE the poetry loving rogue! I hope you do too! So glad they found their perfect match!

Did you miss the first book in the Whispers of the Ton series? Here it is! The Truth about the Earl Read a few pages ahead to see a Sneek Peak!

MY DEAR READER

Thank you for reading and supporting my books! I hope this story brought you some escape from the real world into the always captivating Regency world. A good story, especially one with a happy ending, just brightens your day and makes you feel good! If you enjoyed the book, would you leave a review on Amazon? Reviews are always appreciated.

Below is a complete list of all my books! Why not click and see if one of them can keep you entertained for a few hours?

The Duke's Daughters Series
The Duke's Daughters: A Sweet Regency Romance Boxset
A Rogue for a Lady
My Restless Earl
Rescued by an Earl
In the Arms of an Earl
The Reluctant Marquess (Prequel)

A Smithfield Market Regency Romance
The Smithfield Market Romances: A Sweet Regency Romance Boxset
The Rogue's Flower

Saved by the Scoundrel
Mending the Duke
The Baron's Malady

The Returned Lords of Grosvenor Square
The Returned Lords of Grosvenor Square: A Regency Romance Boxset
The Waiting Bride
The Long Return
The Duke's Saving Grace
A New Home for the Duke

The Spinsters Guild
The Spinsters Guild: A Sweet Regency Romance Boxset
A New Beginning
The Disgraced Bride
A Gentleman's Revenge
A Foolish Wager
A Lord Undone

Convenient Arrangements
Convenient Arrangements: A Regency Romance Collection
A Broken Betrothal
In Search of Love
Wed in Disgrace
Betrayal and Lies
A Past to Forget
Engaged to a Friend

Landon House

Landon House: A Regency Romance Boxset
Mistaken for a Rake
A Selfish Heart
A Love Unbroken
A Christmas Match
A Most Suitable Bride
An Expectation of Love

Second Chance Regency Romance
Second Chance Regency Romance Boxset
Loving the Scarred Soldier
Second Chance for Love
A Family of her Own
A Spinster No More

Soldiers and Sweethearts
Soldiers and Sweethearts Boxset
To Trust a Viscount
Whispers of the Heart
Dare to Love a Marquess
Healing the Earl
A Lady's Brave Heart

Ladies on their Own: Governesses and Companions
Ladies on their Own Boxset
More Than a Companion
The Hidden Governess
The Companion and the Earl
More than a Governess
Protected by the Companion

Lost Fortunes, Found Love
Lost Fortunes, Found Love Boxset
A Viscount's Stolen Fortune
For Richer, For Poorer
Her Heart's Choice
A Dreadful Secret
Their Forgotten Love
His Convenient Match

Only for Love
The Heart of a Gentleman
A Lord or a Liar
The Earl's Unspoken Love
The Viscount's Unlikely Ally
The Highwayman's Hidden Heart
Miss Millington's Unexpected Suitor

Waltzing with Wallflowers
The Wallflower's Unseen Charm
The Wallflower's Midnight Waltz
Wallflower Whispers
The Ungainly Wallflower
The Determined Wallflower
The Wallflower's Secret (Revenge of the Wallflowers series)
The Wallflower's Choice

Whispers of the Ton
The Truth about the Earl
The Truth about the Rogue

Christmas Stories
The Uncatchable Earl
Love and Christmas Wishes: Three Regency Romance Novellas
A Family for Christmas
Mistletoe Magic: A Regency Romance
Heart, Homes & Holidays: A Sweet Romance Anthology

Christmas Kisses Series
Christmas Kisses Box Set
The Lady's Christmas Kiss
The Viscount's Christmas Queen
Her Christmas Duke

Happy Reading!
All my love,
Rose

A SNEAK PEEK OF THE TRUTH ABOUT THE EARL

PROLOGUE

"I was very sorry to hear of the death of your husband."

Lady Norah Essington gave the older lady a small smile, which she did not truly feel. "I thank you. You are very kind." Her tone was dull but Norah had no particular concerns as regarded either how she sounded or how she appeared to the lady. She was, yet again, alone in the world, and as things stood, was uncertain as to what her future would be.

"You did not care for him, I think."

Norah's gaze returned to Lady Gillingham's with such force, the lady blinked in surprise and leaned back a fraction in her chair.

"I mean no harm by such words, I assure you. I –"

"You have made an assumption, Lady Gillingham, and I would be glad if you should keep such notions to yourself." Norah lifted her chin but heard her voice wobble. "I should prefer to mourn the loss of my husband without whispers or gossip chasing around after me."

Lady Gillingham smiled, reached forward, and settled one hand over Norah's. "But of course."

Norah turned her head, trying to silently signal that the meeting was now at an end. She was not particularly well acquainted with the lady and, as such, would be glad of her departure so that she might sit alone and in peace. Besides which, if Lady Gillingham had been as bold as to make such a claim as that directly to Norah herself, then what would she think to say to the *ton*? Society might be suddenly full of whispers about Norah and her late husband—and then what would she do?

"I have upset you. Forgive me."

Norah dared a glance at Lady Gillingham, taking in the gentle way her eyes searched Norah's face and the small, soft smile on her lips. "I do not wish you to disparage my late husband, Lady Gillingham. Nor do I want to hear such rumors being spread in London – whenever it would be that I would have cause to return."

"I quite understand, and I can assure you I do not have any intention of speaking of any such thing to anyone in society."

"Then why state such a thing in my presence? My husband is only a sennight gone and, as I am sure you are aware, I am making plans to remove myself to his estate."

"Provided you are still welcome there."

Norah closed her eyes, a familiar pain flashing through her heart. "Indeed." Suddenly, she wanted very much for Lady Gillingham to take her leave. This was not at all what she had thought would occur. The lady, she had assumed, would simply express her sympathies and take her leave.

"Again, I have injured you." Lady Gillingham let out a long sigh and then shook her head. "Lady Essington, forgive me. I am speaking out of turn and with great thoughtlessness, which I must apologize for. The truth is, I come here out of genuine concern for you, given that I have been in the very same situation."

Norah drew her eyebrows together. She was aware that Lady Gillingham was widowed but did not know when such a thing had taken place.

"I was, at that time, given an opportunity which I grasped at with both hands. It is a paid position but done most discreetly."

Blinking rapidly, Norah tried to understand what Lady Gillingham meant. "I am to be offered employment?" She shook her head. "Lady Gillingham, that is most kind of you but I assure you I will be quite well. My husband often assured me his brother is a kind, warm-hearted gentleman and I have every confidence that he will take care of me." This was said with a confidence Norah did not truly feel but given the strangeness of this first meeting, she was doing so in an attempt to encourage Lady Gillingham to take her leave. Her late husband had, in fact, warned her about his brother on more than one occasion, telling her he was a selfish, arrogant sort who would not care a jot for anyone other than himself.

"I am very glad to hear of it, but should you find yourself in any difficulty, then I would beg of you to consider this. I have written for the paper for some time and find myself a little less able to do so nowadays. The truth is, Lady Essington, I am a little dull when it comes to society and very little takes place that could be of any real interest to anyone, I am sure."

Growing a little frustrated, Norah spread her hands. "I do not understand you, Lady Gillingham. Perhaps this is not -"

"An opportunity to *write*, Lady Essington." Lady Gillingham leaned forward in her chair, her eyes suddenly dark and yet sparkling at the same time. "To write about society! Do you understand what I mean?"

Norah shook her head but a small twist of interest flickered in her heart. "No, Lady Gillingham. I am afraid I do not."

The lady smiled and her eyes held fast to Norah's. "*The London Chronicle*, as you know, has society pages. I am sure you have read them?"

Norah nodded slowly, recalling the times she and her mother had pored over the society pages in search of news as to which gentlemen might be worth considering when it came to her future. "I have found them very informative."

"Indeed, I am glad to hear so." Lady Gillingham smiled as if she had something to do with the pages themselves. "There is a rather large column within the society pages that mayhap you have avoided if you are averse to gossip and the like."

Norah shifted uncomfortably in her chair. The truth was, she *had* read them many times over and had been a little too eager to know of the gossip and rumors swirling through London society whilst, at the same time, refusing to speak of them to anyone else for fear of spreading further gossip.

"I can see you understand what it is I am speaking about. Well, Lady Essington, you must realize that someone writes such a column, I suppose?" She smiled and Norah nodded slowly. "*I* am that person."

Shock spread through Norah's heart and ice filled her chest. Not all of the gossip she had read had been pleasant – indeed, some of it had been so very unfavorable that reputations had been quite ruined.

"You are a little surprised but I must inform you I have set a great deal of trust in you by revealing this truth." Lady Gillingham's smile had quite faded and instead, Norah was left with a tight-lipped older lady looking back at her with steel in her dark eyes.

"I – I understand."

"Good." Lady Gillingham smiled but there was no lightness in her expression. "The reason I speak to you so, Lady Essington, is to offer you the opportunity in the very same way that I was all those years ago."

For some moments, Norah stared at Lady Gillingham with undisguised confusion. She had no notion as to what the lady meant nor what she wanted and, as such, could only shake her head.

Lady Gillingham sighed. "I am tired of writing my column, Lady Essington. As I have said, it is a paid position and all done very discreetly. I wish to return to my little house in the country and enjoy being away in the quiet countryside rather than the hubbub of London. The funds I have received for writing this particular column have been more than enough over the years and I have managed to save a good deal so that I might retire to the country in comfort."

"I see." Still a little confused, Norah twisted her lips to one side for a few moments. "And you wish for *me* to write this for you?"

"For yourself!" Lady Gillingham flung her hands in the air. "They want to continue the column, for it is *very* popular, and as such, they require someone to write it. I thought that, since you find yourself in much the same situation as I was some years ago, you might be willing to think on it."

Blowing out a long, slow breath, Norah found herself nodding out but quickly stopped it from occurring. "I think I should like to consider it a little longer."

"But of course. You have your mourning period, and thereafter, perhaps you might be willing to give me an answer?"

Norah frowned. "But that is a little over a year away."

"Yes, I am well aware it is a long time, Lady Essington. But I shall finish writing for this Season in the hope that you will take over thereafter. It is, as I am sure you have been able to tell, quite secretive and without any danger."

Norah gave her a small smile, finding her heart flooding with a little relief. "Because you are Mrs. Fullerton," she answered, as Lady Gillingham beamed at her. "You write as Mrs. Fullerton, I should say."

"Indeed, I do. I must, for else society would not wish to have me join them in anything, and then where would I be?" A murmur of laughter broke from her lips as she got to her feet, bringing her prolonged visit to an end. "Consider what I have suggested, my dear. I do not know what your circumstances are at present and I am quite certain you will *not* be aware of them until you return to the late Lord Essington's estate but I am quite sure you would do excellently. You may, of course, write to me whenever you wish with any questions or concerns that I could answer for you."

"I very much appreciate your concern *and* your consideration, Lady Gillingham." Rising to her feet, Norah gave the lady a small curtsy, which was returned. "I shall take the year to consider it."

"Do." Reaching out, Lady Gillingham grasped Norah's hands and held them tightly, her eyes fixed on Norah's. "Do not permit yourself to be pushed aside, Lady Essington. Certain characters might soon determine that you do not deserve what is written on Lord Essington's will but be aware that it cannot be contested. Take what is yours and make certain you do all you can for your comfort. No one will take from you what is rightfully yours, I assure you."

Norah's smile slipped and she could only nod as Lady Gillingham squeezed her hands. She was rather fearful of returning to her late husband's estate and being informed of her situation as regarded her husband's death.

"And you must promise me that you will not speak of this to anyone."

"Of course," Norah promised without hesitation. "I shall not tell a soul, Lady Gillingham. Of that, you can be quite certain."

"Good, I am glad." With another warm smile, Lady Gillingham dropped Norah's hands and made her way to the door. "Good afternoon, Miss Essington. I do hope your sorrow passes quickly."

Norah nodded and smiled but did not respond. Did Lady Gillingham know Norah had never had a kind thought for her husband? That their marriage had been solely because of Lord Essington's desire to have a young, pretty wife by his side rather than due to any real or genuine care or consideration for her? Telling herself silently that such a thing did not matter, Norah waited until Lady Gillingham had quit the room before flopping back into her chair and blowing out a long breath.

Most extraordinary. Biting her lip, Norah considered what Lady Gillingham had offered her. Was it something she would consider? Would she become the next writer of the *London Chronicle* society column? It was employment, but not something Norah could simply ignore.

"I might very well require some extra coin," she murmured to herself, sighing heavily as another rap came at the door. Most likely, this would be another visitor coming to express their sympathy and sorrow. Whilst Norah did not begrudge them, she was finding herself rather weary.

I have a year to consider, she reminded herself, calling for the footman to come into the room. *One year. And then I may very well find myself as the new Mrs. Fullerton.*

CHAPTER ONE

One year later.
Taking the hand of her coachman, Norah descended from the carriage and drew in a long breath.

I am back in London.

The strange awareness that she was quite alone – without companion or chaperone – rushed over her, rendering Norah a little uncomfortable. Wriggling her shoulders a little in an attempt to remove such feelings from herself, Norah put a smile on her face and began to walk through St James' Park, praying that Lady Gillingham would be waiting as she had promised.

The last year had been something of a dull one and it brought Norah a good deal of pleasure to be back in town. Society had been severely lacking and the only other people in the world she had enjoyed conversation with had been her lady's maid, Cherry, and the housekeeper. Both had seemed to recognize that Norah was a little lonely and as the months had passed, a semblance of friendship – albeit a strange one – had begun to flourish. However, upon her return to town, Norah had been forced to leave both the maid and the housekeeper behind, for she was no longer permitted to reside in the small estate that had been hers for the last year. Now, she was to find a way to settle in London and with an entirely new complement of staff.

"Ah, Lady Essington! I am so glad to see you again."

Lady Gillingham rose quickly from where she had been seated on the small, wooden bench and, much to Norah's surprise, grasped her hands tightly whilst looking keenly into her eyes.

"I do hope you are well?"

Norah nodded, a prickling running down her spine. "I am quite well, I thank you."

"You have been looked after this past year?"

Opening her mouth to say that yes, she was quite satisfied, Norah slowly closed it again and saw the flicker of understanding in Lady Gillingham's eye.

"The newly titled Lord Essington did not wish for me to reside with him so I was sent to the dower house for the last few months," she explained, as Lady Gillingham's jaw tightened. "I believe that Lord Essington has spent the time attempting to find a way to remove from me what my late husband bequeathed but he has been unable to do so."

Lady Gillingham's eyes flared and a small smile touched the corner of her mouth. "I am very glad to hear it."

"I have a residence here in London and a small

complement of staff." It was not quite the standard she was used to but Norah was determined to make the best of it. "I do not think I shall be able to purchase any new gowns - although it may be required of me somehow – but I am back in town, at the very least."

Lady Gillingham nodded, turned, and began to walk along the path, gesturing for Norah to fall into step with her. "You were given only a small yearly allowance?"

Norah shrugged one shoulder lightly. "It is more than enough to take care of my needs, certainly."

"But not enough to give you any real ease."

Tilting her head, Norah considered what she said, then chose to push away her pride and nod.

"It is as you say." There would be no additional expenses, no new gowns, gloves, or bonnets and she certainly could not eat extravagantly but at least she had a comfortable home. "The will stated that I was to have the furnished townhouse in London and that my brother-in-law is liable for all repairs to keep it to a specific standard for the rest of my remaining life and that, certainly, is a comfort."

"I can see that it is, although might you consider marrying again?"

Norah hesitated. "It is not something I have given a good deal of thought to, Lady Gillingham. I have had a great deal of loss these last few years, with the passing of my mother shortly after my marriage and, thereafter, the passing of Lord Essington himself. To find myself now back in London without a parent or husband is a little strange, and I confess that I find it a trifle odd. However, for the moment, it is a freedom that I wish to explore rather than remove from myself in place of another marriage."

Lady Gillingham laughed and the air around them seemed to brighten. "I quite understand. I, of course, never married again and there is not always a desire to do so, regardless. That is quite an understandable way of thinking and you must allow yourself time to become accustomed to your new situation."

"Yes, I think you are right."

Tilting her head slightly, Lady Gillingham looked sidelong at Norah. "And have you given any consideration to my proposal?"

Norah hesitated, her stomach dropping. Until this moment, she had been quite determined that she would *not* do as Lady Gillingham had asked, whereas now she was no longer as certain. Realizing she would have to live a somewhat frugal life for the rest of her days *or* marry a gentleman with a good deal more fortune – which was, of course, somewhat unlikely since she was a widow – the idea of earning a little more coin was an attractive one.

"I – I was about to refuse until this moment. But now that I am back in your company, I feel quite changed."

Lady Gillingham's eyes lit up. "Truthfully?"

Letting out a slightly awkward laugh, Norah nodded. "Although I am not certain I shall have the same way with words as you. How do you find such interesting stories?"

The burst of laughter that came from Lady Gillingham astonished Norah to the point that her steps slowed significantly.

"Oh, forgive me, Lady Essington! It is clear you have not plunged the depths of society as I have."

A slow flush of heat crept up Norah's cheeks. "It is true that I was very well protected from any belligerent gentlemen and the like. My mother was most fastidious."

"As she ought." Lady Gillingham attempted to hide her smile but it fought to remain on her lips. "But you shall find society a very different beast now, Lady Essington!"

Norah shivered, not certain that she liked that particular remark.

"You are a widowed lady, free to do as you please and act as you wish. You will find that both the gentlemen and ladies of the *ton* will treat you very differently now and that, Lady Essington, is where you will find all manner of stories being brought to your ears."

"I see."

A small frown pulled at Lady Gillingham's brow. "However, I made certain any stories I wrote had a basis in fact. I do not like to spread rumors unnecessarily. I stayed far from stories that would bring grave injury to certain parties."

Norah nodded slowly, seeing the frown and realizing just how seriously Lady Gillingham had taken her employment.

"There is a severe responsibility that must be considered before you take this on, Lady Essington. You must be aware that whatever you write *will* have consequences."

Pressing her lips together tightly, Norah thought about this for a few moments. "I recall that my mother and I used to read the society papers very carefully indeed, to make certain we would not keep company with any gentlemen who were considered poorly by the *ton*."

Lady Gillingham nodded. "Indeed, that is precisely what I mean. If a lady had been taken advantage of, then I would never write about her for fear of what that might entail. However, I would make mention of the gentleman in question, in some vague, yet disparaging, way that made certain to keep the rest of the debutantes away from him."

"I understand."

"We may not be well acquainted, Lady Essington, but I have been told of your kind and sweet nature by others. I believe they thought very well of your mother and, in turn, of you."

Norah put her hand to her heart, an ache in her throat. "I thank you."

Lady Gillingham smiled softly. "So what say you, Lady Essington? Will you do as I have long hoped?"

"Will I write under the name of Mrs. Fullerton?" A slow, soft smile pulled at her lips as she saw Lady Gillingham nod. "And when would they wish their first piece?"

Lady Gillingham shrugged. "I write every week about what I have discovered. Sometimes the article is rather long and sometimes it is very short. The amount you write does not matter. It is what it contains that is of interest. They will pay you the same amount, regardless."

"They?" Norah pricked up her ears at the mention of money. "And might I ask how much is being offered?"

Norah's eyes widened as Lady Gillingham told her of the very large amount that would be given to her for every piece written. *That would allow me to purchase one new gown at the very least!*

"And it is the man in charge of the *London Chronicle* that has asked me for this weekly contribution. In time, you will be introduced to him. But that is only if you are willing to take on the role?"

Taking in a deep breath, Norah let it out slowly and closed her eyes for a moment. "Yes, I think I shall."

Lady Gillingham clapped her hands together in delight, startling a nearby blackbird. "How wonderful! I shall, of course, be glad to assist you with your first article. Thereafter, I fully intend to return to my house in the countryside and remain far away from *all* that London society has to offer." Her smile faded as she spoke, sending a stab of worry into Norah's heart. Could it be that after years of writing such articles, of being in amongst society and seeing all that went on, Lady Gillingham was weary of the *ton*? Norah swallowed hard and tried to push her doubts away. This was to bring her a little more coin and, therefore, a little more ease. After all that she had endured these last few years, that would be of the greatest comfort to her.

"So, when are you next to go into society?"

Norah looked at Lady Gillingham. "I have only just come to London. I believe I have an invitation to Lord Henderson's ball tomorrow evening, however."

"As have I." Lady Gillingham looped her arm through Norah's, as though they were suddenly great friends. "We shall attend together and I will help you find not only what you are to write about but I shall also introduce you to various gentlemn and ladies that you might wish to befriend."

A little confused, Norah frowned. "For what purpose?"

"Oh, some gentlemen, in particular, will have *excellent* potential when it comes to your writings. You do not have to like them – indeed, it is best if you do *not*, for your conscience's sake."

Norah's spirits dropped low. Was this truly the right thing for her to be doing? She did not want to injure gentlemen and ladies unnecessarily, nor did she want to have guilt on her conscience. *But the money would be so very helpful.*

"I can choose what I write, yes?"

Lady Gillingham glanced over at her sharply. "Yes, of course."

"And the newspaper will not require me to write any falsehoods?"

Lady Gillingham shook her head. "No, indeed not."

Norah set her shoulders. "Then I shall do as you have done and write what I think is only best for society to know, in order to protect debutantes and the like from any uncouth gentlemen."

"That is fair." Lady Gillingham smiled and Norah took in a long breath, allowing herself to smile as she settled the matter with her conscience. "I am sure you shall do very well indeed, Lady Essington."

Norah tilted her head up toward the sky for a moment as a sense of freedom burst over her once again.

"I must hope so, Lady Gillingham. The ball will be a very interesting evening indeed, I am sure."

I THINK the society column will yield some very interesting stories, don't you? I hope Lady Essington does well! Check out the rest of the story in the Kindle Store The Truth about the Earl

JOIN MY MAILING LIST

Sign up for my newsletter to stay up to date on new releases, contests, giveaways, freebies, and deals!

Free book with signup!

Monthly Facebook Giveaways! Books and Amazon gift cards!
Join me on Facebook: https://www.facebook.com/rosepearsonauthor

Website: www.RosePearsonAuthor.com

Follow me on Goodreads: Author Page

Printed in Great Britain
by Amazon